Fielder from Nowhere

BY JACKSON SCHOLZ

Batter Up

Fielder from Nowhere

JACKSON SCHOLZ

FIELDER FROM NOWHERE

Morrow Junior Books • New York

First published in 1948 by Morrow Junior Books.
Reissued by both Morrow Junior Books and Beech Tree Books in 1993
with changes that update the text for contemporary readers.

Printed in the United States of America.

1 2 3 4 5 6 7 8 9 10

Library of Congress Cataloging-in-Publication Data
Scholz, Jackson.
Fielder from nowhere / Jackson Scholz.
p. cm.
Summary: A professional baseball player organizes baseball games
for boys in the inner city but almost loses his career and the
support of the boys because of a grim reminder of his past.
ISBN 0-688-12486-0
[1. Baseball—Fiction.] I. Title. PZ7.S37Fh 1993
[Fic]—dc20 92-32797 CIP AC

Fielder from Nowhere

1

It's a long trip from California to Florida. It's longer still when a fellow leaves the coast with five lonesome dollars in his pocket. Motorists are wary of hitchhikers, railroad brakemen are on the lookout for people who want free rides, and jobs are scarce for drifters.

Ken Holt made the trip just the same. He worked when he could, ate when he could, and traveled when he could. He arrived in Seminole City, Florida, a month and a half after shaking the dust of California from his heels.

He wasn't much to look at when he pulled into town. His dark, shapeless suit was stiff with the dirt of many boxcars. The seams of his shoes were split, and inner soles of cardboard protected his feet from the hot ground. He needed a haircut and a shave. He needed a bath, too.

The straight set of his shoulders, however, was not in keeping with his clothes. Neither was the purposeful reach of his stride. In further contrast was the hard line of his jaw, the forward stubborn thrust of his head.

He was walking through a residential district when an approaching policeman gave him a careful scrutiny and then stopped him.

"We know what to do with bums in this town," the man said without preamble.

Ken looked straight at him. Ken's eyes were smoky-blue and full of challenge.

"You ought to know," he conceded. "That's your job."

The policeman apparently hadn't expected an answer of this sort. He cast a speculative eye upon Ken's height, his breadth of shoulder, and his length of arm. Then he shifted his puzzled look to the battered, imitation leather suitcase Ken was carrying.

"What've you got in there?" he demanded.

"Not that it's any of your business," Ken said, "but I've got a baseball outfit. I'm heading for the Terriers' camp. Where can I find it?"

The policeman wasn't so sure of himself now. The local Chamber of Commerce had gone to some pains to induce the big-league Philadelphia Terriers to use Seminole City for their spring training quarters. Also, some rookies had already shown up, hopeful of berths on old Jake Tobin's team.

The man scratched his chin and admitted grudgingly, "I guess that makes a difference. Follow this street for three blocks, turn right, and you'll see the ballpark."

Ken nodded and started on his way. A recent rain had left puddles in the gutters of the street. Ken heard a car approaching swiftly from behind him but paid no attention to it until the wheels of the car slashed through a puddle near the sidewalk, showering him with a sheet of muddy water.

Nothing of that nature could have hurt Ken's clothes, but his feelings were a different matter. Already hanging by a slender thread, his temper snapped. He saw the back of a green convertible, its top down. He saw the big head and the bulky shoulders of the driver. "Hey! You clumsy jerk!"

The tires of the car squealed as the driver applied the brakes. He jammed the gears into reverse, whipped back to where Ken stood, and stopped.

Ken saw a heavy-featured dark face, the face of a man who could make quick enemies and hold them doggedly. A man of this type, Ken knew, could be dangerous, a fact which suited him right now.

"Were you yellin' at *me,* bud?"

"How'd you guess it?" Ken snarled back at him. "Why don't you watch where you're driving? What's the idea of splatterin' me with mud?"

"To start with, guy, I didn't *know* I'd splattered you. I didn't do it on purpose. So much for that. The rest is, I don't like to be called a jerk."

He fished in his pocket, pulled out a dollar bill, wadded it up and tossed it on the ground in front of Ken. "Get your suit cleaned and pressed, if you can call that thing a suit. And after this be careful of your language."

Ken stepped on the bill carefully, ground it into the soil with his heel, and said, "Get out of that car, you ugly ape. I'll teach you a few manners."

The other man needed no second invitation. He exploded with a well-coordinated speed that brought him out of the car in an instant. He came at Ken, who was waiting with pleasure. But before the battle could be joined, a loud voice bellowed, "Hold it! Take it easy, there!"

It was the policeman again. He hurried up and stepped between the pair. "This bum troublin' you, Mr. Borg?"

Something drilled through the anger in Ken's mind. Borg? It couldn't be. Yet—Ken took a closer look—it was Cy Borg, right fielder of the Terriers. Ken had seen his picture many times.

The discovery did not make Ken any more kindly disposed toward Borg. He was still sorry the policeman had interfered. He heard Borg say, "He's not troubling *me,* officer. But you sure got here in time to save his hide."

"Shall I run him in, Mr. Borg?" Then he added as an afterthought, "He said he was on his way to the Terrier camp. Says he's a baseball player."

Borg studied Ken Holt with a new and slightly predatory interest. A tight look of amusement came upon his face. "No, officer, let him go. It'll make me glad to know I haven't seen the last of him. He's got a lot to learn."

"Just as you say, Mr. Borg," the policeman said. "Get goin', you!"

The last was addressed to Ken, who, with an effort, kept his mouth shut and followed the advice. He picked up his suitcase and started off. Borg climbed into his car and roared away.

As Ken approached the field he felt his pulses quicken. He forgot his anger toward Cy Borg. He also forgot some of his weariness and hunger. This was the end of the road. At least he hoped it was. He had struggled hard enough to get here.

He didn't have the fifty-cent admission fee, so he avoided the turnstiles and followed the fence to the players' gate. The gatekeeper, an old man with moth-eaten whiskers, eyed him sourly, drew gurgling noises from a battered pipe, and said ungraciously, "Another rookie, huh?"

Ken nodded.

"Got a pass from the manager, Jake Tobin?"

"No."

"He expecting you?"

"No."

"Too bad."

"You mean I can't get in?"

"That's what I mean, sonny. If you want to see Jake, you'll have to see him outside the park."

Ken felt his anger begin to stir again. It was the

unreasonable, pettish anger of frustration. He was tired to the inside of his bones, and his stomach felt as hollow as a tennis ball. It seemed incredibly unfair that he should have reached this point only to be balked by an obdurate old man.

He could, of course, follow his advice and approach Tobin somewhere outside the ballpark. But that wasn't what he wanted or the way he had planned it. His stubbornness welled up, but he was smart enough to recognize a stubbornness in the old man equal to his own.

Ken smothered his useless anger, smoothed the muscles of his face, and set his suitcase on the ground. He tried to figure a strategic opening and, stalling for time, he wiped his perspiring forehead with a blue bandanna handkerchief.

The gatekeeper, ignoring Ken, pulled on his pipe. It squealed and spluttered. He removed it from his mouth, gazed at it accusingly, then returned it to his mouth and applied a match.

The act of lighting up brought both of the old man's hands into Ken's line of vision. He regarded them casually at first, then with quickened interest as an idea clicked in his mind. The fingers of the right hand were gnarled and bent, those of the left hand comparatively straight. Ken played a hunch and said, "You've spent plenty of hours behind a plate."

"Eh?" said the other, caught off guard and permitting the match an involuntary jerk. He steadied his hand, got the pipe working to his satisfaction, and inquired, "What makes you think so?"

"Your right hand. I'll bet you've stopped plenty of foul tips with it."

The old fellow raised his hand and regarded it with fond pride. "You guessed right, sonny," he admitted. "It took a lot of tips to fix it up like this. Old Pete Blake, that's me, has seen a lot of balls come down the groove."

Ken estimated Blake's age at close to eighty, coupled it with his own wide knowledge of baseball history, then played another hunch. He said, "It took a real man to play backstop in those days, with the pitcher blazing 'em in from fifty feet away. They didn't change the distance to sixty and a half feet until 1893, did they?"

A grudging admiration began to show in Pete Blake's eyes. He still tried to maintain his hard-boiled front, but was waging a losing battle. "That's when they changed it, sonny. But they didn't have to change it for guys like me. We could take it. It was the batters who couldn't stand the pressure."

He eyed Ken with the expression of a schoolteacher who was about to pass or flunk a student on the strength of the next answer. "And who," he demanded, "was the pitcher who *I* think made 'em change the distance, the man who could burn 'em in so fast from fifty feet that the batters couldn't see 'em?"

It was not a matter of mind reading so far as Ken Holt was concerned, but a matter of simple calculation and memory of statistics. "Cy Young, the greatest of 'em all."

The answer shattered Pete Blake's last reserve. He cackled delightedly. "That's him!" he yelped. "The greatest of 'em all."

"You bet," said Ken, pushing his luck, and grateful that Cy Young happened to be one of his own heroes, with whose record he was familiar. "He played for twenty-two years. He pitched in eight hundred seventy-three games, which, of course, included relief pitching, but he won five hundred and eleven and lost three hundred and fifteen for a lifetime percentage of .619."

Blake was frankly admiring now. "You know

your baseball history, sonny. What position do you play?"

"Outfield."

"Any good at it?"

"That's what I'm trying to find out." Ken grinned.

"All right, all right," said old Blake peevishly. "You sneaked in a punch when I wasn't lookin', and don't think I don't know it. Go on inside. Jake Tobin'll tear my head off, but I hope he tears yours off first. Get goin' before I change my mind."

Ken picked up his suitcase, passed through the gate, and said, "Thanks, Mr. Blake, thanks a lot."

"Shut up," growled Blake.

Ken entered the ballpark, trying to keep the tension from his nerves. This, indeed, was the end of his long journey, but the hardest part was still ahead, the important part. Misgivings tried to worm their way into his thoughts. He fought them down. This was no time for doubt, no time to let a feeling of inferiority creep in. He tried to tell himself he was as good as any Terrier upon the field.

He had seen enough pictures of Jake Tobin to recognize him easily. He was standing near the dugout, feet apart, hands on his hips. He was old in years but young in vitality. Twenty-three years of managing the tough Terriers would have broken an ordinary man.

Tobin, however, was not ordinary. He thrived on baseball, as evidenced by the sound muscles of his stocky body, and his ruddy bulldog face. He had carried the Terriers to more than their share of pennants.

It was well known in baseball circles that Jake Tobin was not always in a genial frame of mind, and this appeared to be one of his ferocious days. The Brickyard Gang, as the Terriers were often called, did not always respond to love and kindness. They had to be fed a little brimstone now and then, and Tobin was the man to do it.

Ken recognized the storm signals too late. He couldn't have backed out now if he had wanted to, which he didn't. The doggedness of purpose that had brought him to this point was still with him. He approached Tobin from the side and plunked his suitcase on the ground.

Tobin heard the thud of the suitcase and turned sharply from the business of bawling out the Terrier first baseman. His eyes narrowed as they came to rest on Ken's untidiness. He chewed off the end of his dead cigar, spat the fragments to the ground, and said, "No handouts today. Scram!"

"I don't want your charity," Ken snapped back. "I want a job on your team."

It was big talk, but Ken Holt was playing another hunch, this time a desperate one. He sensed that he could only gain Tobin's attention by punching his words in, and in this he appeared to be partly right.

Old Jake stared as if he couldn't believe his ears. He seemed jolted to the point where he obviously forgot the important matter of how this fresh kid had managed to get into the ballpark. Then his expression changed, became almost benign. His voice took on a soft, disarming tone.

"Well now, that's my mistake, son," he apologized. "And just what position did you have in mind? They're all open, you understand. I'll be more than glad to bench any of these beanbag tossers to make a place for you. Just say the word and the position's yours."

Ken kept his eyes steady upon Tobin's and said bluntly, "You sold yourself short on outfielders this year, and you need a good one. Anyone who follows baseball knows it. You've also got to plug a big hole in your batting list."

Jake Tobin was doing a manful job of keeping his temper. Ken sensed it wouldn't hold much longer. The Brickyard Gang was drawing closer to enjoy the show.

"Listen, my dirty young friend, whoever you are," said Tobin patiently, "rookies are a dime a dozen around here. I turn 'em away in batches, because I like to pick my own." His voice began to get away from him, gaining height and volume. It finally broke into a roar. "And *you,* so help me, are the cockiest young punk of 'em all!"

"Mr. Tobin," Ken Holt said quietly, "I've got to be cocky." A touch of desperation was creeping uncontrollably into his tone. "I've come all the way from . . ." He bit off the sentence sharply. "I've come a long way for a tryout with the Terriers. All I want is a chance to show you."

Tobin chewed hard upon the end of his cigar. He tried to maintain his expression of ferocity, but it was too much for him. Suddenly he thrust both arms toward heaven. "I'm a sucker," he told the world at large. "I ought to found an orphan asylum. I'm a pushover for a hard-luck yarn. All right, kid, let's get it over with. Then I'll feed you and send you on your way. Got an outfit?"

Ken nodded. He hadn't meant to pull a hard-luck yarn, and he didn't like the amused grins of the Brickyard Gang.

He carried his suitcase to one side, opened it, and took out a pair of baseball shoes and a fielder's mitt. He didn't bother with the uniform, from which all identifying marks had been carefully removed. He shed his coat, sat on the grass to don his shoes, got up, and announced that he was ready.

Tobin's eyes strayed toward the shabby glove and showed approval. There was no padding in the palm, and the fingers wabbled limply. A real ball player had lavished care and tenderness upon that mitt. Then Tobin grunted, as if aware of his temporary weakness.

"Anyone can own a glove," he said testily, "but not everybody can use one. Get out in the field. Give me a fungo bat and a ball, somebody."

2

K*en tried to limber* up as he jogged to center field. He was a trifle alarmed at the weakness of his legs. He had missed too many meals, a matter he didn't care to dwell upon right now.

Tobin, probably resenting his momentary softness, decided to end things as soon as possible. No sooner had Ken turned to face him than Tobin boosted a long fungo intended for the wide open spaces near the fence.

The horsehide would have reached those open spaces, too, if Ken had not started moving at the crack of the bat. He didn't stop to see where the ball was going; he just got under way as automatically as if someone had pushed a button on his control board. It was as instinctive as breathing.

He knew the wallop was a long one, and he knew he didn't have time to pick any daisies. One lightning glance gave him the direction, and his long legs temporarily carried the responsibility.

Ken was fast. He had to be to reach the spot where he knew that ball would land. Then instinct pushed another button and he turned his head. He caught the white flash of the ball. His hands rose smoothly. The ball zipped in across his shoulder, landed in the mitt, and stayed there.

It was a sweet catch any way you looked at it. Ken knew that a certain amount of luck had entered in, because his timing, of necessity, must have rusted slightly. At any rate he had made it, but he heard no cheers of commendation from the gallery.

He did not make the mistake of trying a long throw until his arm had limbered up a bit. He didn't want to strain a valuable muscle at this stage of the game. His position was too precarious. So he lobbed the ball to the infield where a Terrier retrieved it.

Tobin tried another one. This time it was deliberately short. Ken had to charge it at high speed. It was one of those shoestring catches, the sort a fielder shouldn't try if men were on the bases.

But Ken was handicapped with no restrictions of that kind. He came in hard, leaped forward, and met the ball just off the ground. It slammed into the pocket of his glove. His fingers clamped down hard. He lost his balance, hit the ground, pulled an acrobatic somersault, and came to his feet with the ball still in his mitt. It was a showy catch, but the Terriers remained unmoved.

Then Tobin really went to town. His uncanny skill with the fungo bat was something Ken had heard about but never seen. He saw it now, and soon the breath was rasping through his throat. It became evident that Tobin could practically drop the horsehide on a handkerchief at any point beyond the infield.

Ken could not get all of them, of course. But, driven by his present urgent need, he nailed more than anyone had a right to expect. Then, when his arm got limbered up, he lined a few of them toward the plate. They came in low and fast, reaching the rubber on the second bounce, clean accurate throws that would have made it difficult for a runner trying to score from third.

Tobin finally waved him in, and Ken walked back

on legs he could hardly keep from wobbling. Now that the tension was momentarily over, he wanted to stretch out on the grass and sleep for a week.

When Ken reached the silent group of Terriers, Tobin's face showed nothing. "What's your name?" he asked abruptly.

"Holt. Ken Holt."

Tobin studied him intently for a moment. Ken expected a barrage of questions. He braced himself for a cross-examination that didn't come. Apparently Tobin had some good reason for delaying the inquisition. "Are you as hungry as you look?" he demanded bluntly.

"Probably hungrier."

"Okay, kid. Hike over to the Parker Hotel. Tell 'em I sent you, and tell 'em to put you in the room with Harry Crane. Then get a meal. You can sign the check."

Ken didn't need a second invitation. It had been a long, long time since he had heard such pleasant words. He inquired the address of the hotel and set off in that direction, grimly satisfied. He hadn't made the grade yet, but he knew the first hurdle had been cleared at any rate.

He located the hotel without difficulty. It was a rambling white frame building with an inviting look of coolness. The lawn was wide and filled with palms and flowers. It looked expensive, and Ken had a moment of misgiving as he entered the wide front door.

The feeling, it appeared, was not without foundation. A quartet of bellboys eyed his shabbiness with shocked alarm, but Ken squared his shoulders and strode formidably across the lobby toward the desk.

The dapper room clerk, watching his approach, looked horrified. He might have worn the same expression if someone had led a horse into his lobby. Ken reached the desk, plunked down his suitcase, and snapped, "Tobin sent me."

The effect was magical. The clerk thawed like an ice cube in a blowtorch flame. His stiff face broke into a smile so suddenly Ken wondered why it didn't crack. He shoved forward a registration card and proffered a pen with a swooping gesture of respect.

"Just sign this, sir," he said. "I have accommodations for you."

Ken signed his name. His pen hovered uncertainly over the space requiring his address. He finally wrote in Seminole City and let it go at that. The clerk raised no objection.

"Mr. Tobin wants me in the room with Harry Crane."

The clerk flicked an eye at the registration card, read Ken's name in its upside-down position, and said, "Certainly, Mr. Holt. The boy will show you up. Front!"

A bellhop hurried to the spot, and, taking his cue from the room clerk, picked up the suitcase and preceded Ken with a respectful, "This way, sir."

The bellhop guided him to 416 and departed with the last of Ken's cash, which added up to thirty cents. Ken looked about and found the room a pleasant, airy place, provided with twin beds. It also had a private bath and, seeing it, Ken muttered, "Boy, oh boy!"

He also saw that Harry Crane had harum-scarum notions about neatness. Clothes and personal possessions were scattered far and wide. A pair of shoes were lying on the floor, tremendous brogans.

"Rig one of 'em with oars," mused Ken, "and you'd have a rowboat to go fishing in. At any rate, I'm not rooming with a midget."

He wasted no more time in speculation. He shed

his clothes and hurried into the bathroom with the avidness of a man who had long been denied the luxury of soap and water. He shaved first, then stepped into the shower, grunting with pleasure as he applied the lather, washed it off, then gave himself another coat of suds.

He was hungry enough to eat a bushel of sawdust without salt, but it was some time before he could drag himself from the cool water of the shower. When he finally managed it and pushed the curtain back, he let out another grunt, this time of surprise.

A huge figure was leaning against the doorway of the bathroom, a rawboned man over six feet tall, undoubtedly Harry Crane, the owner of the shoes. Crane confirmed Ken's guess.

"Hi!" he said. "I'm Crane. You're Holt. Glad to know you."

He came forward with a limber motion, extending a huge hand. Ken's hand was big, but Crane's engulfed it easily. Ken studied him with sharp attention. He saw a long, angular face, intelligent blue eyes, and an incredibly long nose.

It was obvious at once that Crane would win no beauty prizes, even against meager competition, but the conviction hit Ken solidly that he was going to like him. Ken grinned and said, "I'm glad to know you, too."

Crane handed him a towel. Ken said, "Thanks, Harry," and started to dry himself.

Crane reestablished himself in the doorway. "Nobody calls me Harry but my mother. Beezer is the name I go by. I come by it honestly, of course. My nose. Quite a snozzle, huh?"

"Not bad," conceded Ken.

Beezer laughed. "I used to be pretty touchy about it," he admitted. "But I found it didn't pay. I've got it for keeps, so I might as well be proud of it."

Back in the room, Ken eyed his dingy clothing with distaste. Beezer rummaged in a drawer and came out with a clean pair of shorts, an undershirt, and a shirt.

"Try these," he said. "You can shorten the shirt sleeves. My arms are a little long, gorilla length. That's where my speed comes from."

Ken accepted the garments gratefully. "Thanks," he said. "I've been traveling pretty light."

"I've traveled light myself at times," admitted Beezer, showing no further interest. "You looked pretty good on the field today."

"I had a little luck. I guess you're a pitcher, aren't you?"

"Yeah. A rookie, temporarily. I'll get a contract, though. I've got the stuff."

Ken shot him a guarded glance.

Beezer caught the look.

"You think I'm cocky, huh? Well, I am," he stated, sparing Ken the necessity of answering the question. "I'm good, and I'd be a chump if I didn't know it. A pitcher's got to be cocky, because he's the mainspring of the team. The other eight guys, whether they admit it or not, are just along for the ride. A club can win with several weak positions in the field, but it can't win with weak pitchers."

Ken smothered a quick surge of resentment. He saw the fallacy of Beezer's reasoning, but sensed that the subject was not open for discussion. He also sensed that a rookie following that line of reasoning was asking for a lot of trouble, but Ken didn't mention that fact either. He did not feel he was qualified to give advice just now.

Beezer expanded upon the subject of his pitching prowess while Ken was dressing. Ken listened and became puzzled at his own reactions. The normal reaction, so he reasoned, would be to dislike the other man heartily. Beezer was a cocky, breezy braggart, yet Ken still liked him.

"How about a little food?" Beezer said.

"Food?" said Ken reflectively. "Food? The word has a familiar sound. I must have heard it somewhere."

"The chow's good here. Let's go."

Ken packed away a meal that left the waitress staring. It was a wonderful experience, eating all he wanted, and when he finally left the dining room he was feeling like a human being for the first time in many months.

The feeling of contentment and security was shortlived. He had known, of course, it would be, accepting the fact that rough weather was ahead. He declined Beezer's invitation to a movie.

"I'd better stick around," said Ken.

"I guess you had," conceded Beezer. "See you later."

So Ken found a chair in a secluded corner of the broad veranda. He was not surprised when Tobin approached him some time later, eased himself into another chair, and said, "We've got to have a talk."

Ken didn't like the idea much, but he had known it was inevitable. He nodded, trying to keep the tenseness from his mind and muscles. Tobin lighted a cigar, blew out a cloud of smoke, and turned to Ken.

"All right, Holt," said Tobin bluntly. "Where're you from?"

"From the West," said Ken conservatively.

"Where'd you learn to play that sort of baseball?"

"I started on the sand lots," admitted Ken, trying to keep out of deep water.

Tobin puffed awhile in silence. "Son," he said at last, "you're stallin' all over the place, and I'm afraid this man-of-mystery stuff won't go around here. You apparently bummed your way east when no less than three major-league teams have their camps out there on the coast. What's the answer?"

"Maybe I like the Terriers," Ken offered.

"No dice, son. If you can handle a bat like you can a glove, you're big-league material, and that doesn't pop up ready-made from sand lots. You've been playing plenty of baseball, yet I've never heard of you. Come again."

Ken hauled in a slow deep breath.

"I'm afraid, Mr. Tobin," he said quietly, "you'll have to let it go at that. This mystery stuff isn't a gag or a racket. The law isn't after me, if that's what you want to know."

"You're holding out plenty," Tobin reminded him. "What's behind all this?"

"A long-range plan of my own, sir," Ken told him with dogged vagueness. "Maybe it'll work out and maybe it won't, but I'm hoping for the chance to give it a try. Maybe I'm all wrong. Maybe I'm going about it the wrong way, but it's the way I see it, and I've got to play the cards I have."

Tobin studied him intently in the dim light, eyeing the stubborn line of his jaw. When Tobin spoke, his voice was gruff but kindly. "I won't put the screws on, son, to make you tell me anything you don't want to. I'll take your word the law's not after you, that you're in the clear. And I *do* need a new outfielder. You were right in that respect. But he can't help me if he can't bat. We'll find that out tomorrow. If you're a flop at the plate, I'm through with you. If you can sock 'em, I'll gamble on you. It's a promise. So you don't have to tell me about yourself unless you want to. Is that fair?"

It was fair, infinitely fairer than anything Ken had expected. He felt a stirring of uneasiness, a feeling that expanded till he felt ungrateful and ashamed. Jake Tobin was willing to give him every possible opportunity to make good with the Terriers, while he, Ken Holt, was unwilling to come clean, unwilling to tell Tobin the things he had a right to know.

Tobin may have read his thoughts. His next words seemed to indicate it. "Don't worry about it, kid, until we see how things work out. If you're no good with a bat, I can't use you on the Terriers. Maybe you'll make the grade. If you do, it'll be time enough to decide then whether you still want to remain a man of mystery."

Ken let his breath out slowly. "Thanks," he said. "I've heard you were a square shooter. Now I know it."

"It pays off," said Tobin dryly.

He arose from his chair, moved away, and left Ken to himself.

3

Ken slept for twelve solid hours that night as if he had been drugged, despite the innumerable things he had to worry him, and awoke the next morning feeling great. He was somewhat stiff from his unaccustomed workout of the day before, but knew his muscles would limber up with a little exercise.

He was concerned primarily with his nerves. They began to tighten up as the hour approached for his second workout with the Terriers. He knew what a long layoff could mean to a man's batting eye, and he also knew that Tobin wouldn't make things easy for him.

Not that Tobin would toss him into the discard after a single unimpressive trip to the plate, but Ken knew the importance of making that first trip impressive. A few solid hits wouldn't hurt his stock at all.

Jake Tobin did not keep him waiting. He assigned players, mostly rookies, to the fielding spots. The manager's attitude was businesslike, impersonal, when he turned to Ken. "Okay, Holt. Pick a bat and get in there."

Ken found a club that suited him, swung it a few times to get the feel of it, then moved toward the batter's box. His nerves were jumping around too much to please him, but he shook his muscles as loose as possible. The Terriers remained outwardly indifferent, but Ken sensed their curious interest as they watched his first appearance at the plate.

There was a rookie on the mound, a college boy named Green, who was trying to climb the steep cliff to a Terriers contract. He seemed as nervous as Ken, which made things even. Truck Hawley, a first-string catcher, was behind the plate. Green squinted for Truck's signal, nodded, and uncorked his fast one. It was too close. Ken pulled his stomach in and let the ball zing past.

Green tried a hook on the next offering. Ken took a conservative cut at it and did not connect squarely. He fouled it on the ground behind first base, but the contact of the ball against his bat sent a welcome tingle up his arms.

He felt better from then on. He had seen more speed and sharper hooks than the pitcher had shown thus far. Green tried another curve. Ken judged the break, stepped in smoothly, and connected. The ball whistled over second base.

He suppressed a grin that did not have much humor in it. He wondered what the Terriers would think if they knew the brand of pitching he had been accustomed to—the sizzling, baffling deliveries of Ozzie Klein, the great hurler who had dropped so suddenly out of big-league baseball.

The memory, depressing as it was, brought confidence to Ken. The kinks began to loosen in his nerves, and the bat began to feel familiar to his hands. He hit three more of Green's deliveries, and one of them went for a certain triple.

At the end of his four clouts he stepped back from the plate, but Tobin called, "Stay in there, Holt!"

Then he added, "Lefty, come out here and toss a few!"

Ken felt a warning quiver travel up his spine. The new pitcher would undoubtedly be Lefty Piper, the Terrier ace who had chalked up twenty-four victories the previous season. It was a name to give cold shudders to any rookie, and Ken was no exception.

Lefty had been warming up on the sideline. He exploded a final fireball in the catcher's mitt. It sounded like the bursting of a hand grenade, and Lefty, nodding approval, hitched up his pants and started toward the pitcher's mound, calmly confident of mowing down the rookie.

It was a bad moment for Ken Holt. His nerves began to play tricks on him again, dragging his thoughts into apprehensive channels. It was not the state of mind a man should have when facing a hurler like Lefty Piper, so Ken stepped from the batter's box, dusted his hands upon the ground, and tried to pull himself together.

He went about it practically. He told himself he was accustomed to the pitching of Ozzie Klein, that Lefty Piper had never reached Klein's heights and probably never would. So far so good. But Ken had to face the fact that his batting eye was somewhat rusty. Still it was early in the season and Lefty's arm was probably not in top-notch shape. Ken had his nerves under control when he stepped back in the batter's box.

Lefty stood upon the mound, relaxed, a big man with an amiable, broad face and steady eyes, superbly confident. He studied Ken a moment, then went into a limber windup and threw.

The ball came in like a fuzzy streak. Ken judged it to be slightly wide, outside. He let it go, then watched the curve break fast to slice in across the plate. An umpire, had there been one, would have called a strike.

Ken felt a hot flush of annoyance. He worked his spikes into the dirt and waited for the next one, trying to imitate Lefty's complete relaxation.

The second pitch was another curve. Ken riveted his eyes on it. Too low. He let it pass. An umpire would have called a ball. Ken felt a little better.

Lefty tried a fast one, and it was fast! Ken could almost hear it whistle. It was slightly high, probably a ball, but the sort of pitch Ken ordinarily would have gone for. He liked them high. He let it go deliberately, playing for a little extra time to study Lefty's style.

Lefty raised his eyebrows in a quizzical expression which implied, Are you going to stand there forever without swinging?

Ken refused to let it bother him. He studied the next windup, and sensed it to be different from the previous ones, a bit more exaggerated.

Ken's brain clicked, warning him, "A change of pace!"

The hunch was good but not quite good enough. The knuckleball came floating at him like a small toy balloon. He could almost count the stitches in the seams. It was a better change of pace than he had expected, but he didn't find it out till after he had swung so hard he almost fell. It was a colossal whiff.

He heard amused snorts from the watching Terriers. One of them said, "Don't look now, but I'll bet he popped the laces in his shoes."

Ken felt ridiculous, but his brain was busy lining up the facts he had learned concerning Lefty's pitching. He had had a chance to study Lefty's curve, his fastball, and his change of pace, and none of them was quite as good as Ozzie Klein's.

But Ken did not underestimate the man out on the mound. Lefty intended to work carefully. It showed in all his motions. There was no smugness there. He studied the batter calmly, undoubtedly remembering that Ken, apparently, did not like high ones.

So Lefty threw a high one. It blazed in level with Ken's chin. Ken moved with smooth coordination. The swing looked almost lazy. He connected, solidly. The ball sprouted wings and disappeared across the left field fence.

When Lefty turned from watching the ball's flight, he regarded Ken with new respect. "Nice wallop, kid. I didn't think you liked 'em up there."

"I'd rather have 'em high," admitted Ken.

"You won't get any more," said Lefty grimly.

The southpaw kept his word. He sent no more high ones down the groove. He settled down to work, paying Ken the subtle compliment of treating him like a dangerous batter. Accepting the challenge, Ken snugged his cleats against the ground and hauled himself into a shell of concentration.

As a right-handed batter, Ken held a definite advantage over a left-handed pitcher, because Lefty's best curves were forced to break toward Ken rather than away from him. He served prompt notice that he did not have to wait for high ones by outguessing a low hook that broke in toward his knees. He swung with a compact, explosive force that sent a roaring grounder to deep short. The rookie shortstop knocked it down. He might have had a play at first and he might not. It could have gone for an infield single.

Lefty worked on Ken carefully, aided by the veteran catcher, Truck Hawley. Ken was pitted against a pair of experts, but refused to let the fact upset him. He held his fire against the bad ones, not always guessing right but striking a fair average.

He went after the good ones, or at least he tried to. He whiffed a few of them, but never made three strikes in a row. He sent four long ones to the outfield, three of which were caught by the fielders. The fourth bounced off the left field wall for a certain double.

He also kept the infield busy. Good fielding robbed him of two possible hits, but he did get two clean ones: one through the pitcher's mound across the second bag and the other between third and short.

It was a competent display of batting power, and Ken was well aware of it when Tobin finally called him from the plate. Truck Hawley tossed him a gruff, "Nice goin', kid." Lefty Piper sent him a rueful but forgiving grin. The other Terriers eyed him with subdued respect but made no overt moves toward friendship. After all, he was just a rookie. He looked good, to be sure, but there was always the chance he might have had two lucky days. Plenty of rookies started well and faded out before the season opened.

Ken started toward the bat pile, trying to keep the satisfaction from his eyes as he approached Jake Tobin. Tobin's attitude was still impersonal. If he was pleased with Ken's showing, his expression didn't show it. He said, "I'll toss you a few more fungos later on."

At the end of batting practice Ken chased fungos. Again he ran head-on into Jake Tobin's deadly skill, but again he caught all the flies he should have had and a lot he could have missed. He was tired but satisfied when Tobin finally called a halt.

The Terriers, as they headed for the showers, were still noncommittal in their attitude toward Ken, but he felt an underlying tolerance that satisfied him. He kept his mouth shut, his expression blank, and made no overtures.

He was not surprised, however, when Cy Borg came up to him in the locker room. On the occasion of their first meeting Ken had, in effect, challenged the big fielder, and a man of Borg's pugnacity would never rest until he had given Ken the chance to carry out his threat.

The present setup was all in Cy Borg's favor. He was playing, so to speak, upon his own home grounds.

Ken was shedding his soggy uniform when Borg came over to him. He stood there, arms akimbo, saying nothing, merely staring. Ken met his unfriendly eyes for several seconds, then, remembering his role as a rookie, dropped his gaze. He propped a foot on the bench and started to unlace his shoe, wondering nervously how far Borg would try to push him. Borg kept him waiting a moment longer, then demanded, "Do you like baseball better'n hoboin'?"

Ken felt the eyes of the other Terriers upon him. He told himself that maybe rookies were supposed to stand a little razzing, and that the Terriers were accepting Borg's overture as a routine attempt to find out whether or not he could take it. Ken took a firm grip on himself and played up.

"I sure do," he said. "It's got it beat a mile."

"Figuring to stay around awhile?" Borg asked.

"I'd sure like to," admitted Ken, not looking up. "If I don't stick around, it won't be because I haven't tried."

"Don't make me laugh," said Borg unpleasantly. "Bums are all alike. Give 'em a handout and they're on the road again before you know they're gone. Anyway, I'm not so sure I'd like to have a tramp playing in the outfield with me."

Ken kept his head because he knew what was going on. He straightened, bringing his eyes on a level with Borg's. "Now look, mister," he said. "I'm not looking for trouble. If I've managed to get in your hair, I'm sorry. All I want is a chance to mind my own business."

"You've already stuck your neck out too far to suit *me,*" said Borg. He turned to the others with the explanation. "I met this bum on the street. We had an argument and he attacked me. A cop interrupted us!" He whirled on Ken again and snapped, "Let's get this matter straight. There's nobody to interrupt us now."

The statement was too optimistic. Ken, by this time, was ready to get things settled, but Borg had overplayed his hand. Truck Hawley lumbered to the spot like a big bear on its hind legs.

"Lay off, Cy," said Hawley bluntly.

Borg whirled on him. "Say, listen," he began. "I—"

"You heard me the first time, Cy," snapped Hawley.

Borg glared at Truck a moment, then shrugged. It was a shrug of frustration rather than defeat. Borg wasn't afraid of Truck, but he recognized the catcher's calm determination.

Borg said, "You're just postponing the thing, Truck."

"Okay," conceded Truck. "But this is not the time or place."

That ended the matter for the moment. Borg moved away and Ken went on with his undressing, glad of the interruption. It had been a close call, too close for comfort. He wouldn't have wanted to start his Terrier career with a locker room brawl—assuming he had a career ahead of him.

He understood, of course, that a showdown was inevitable, but he hoped to postpone it as long as possible, at least until he had gained a firm toehold with the Terriers. It would all depend, of course, on how hard Cy Borg pushed him.

4

Cy Borg did plenty of tenacious pushing in the following days, but always managed to stop just short of the barrier Ken Holt had built around his temper. It was close at times, but Ken kept his self-control and scored a series of nice moral victories.

He was aided in this by the high speed at which Jake Tobin drove the Terriers. Tobin held them at a dizzy pace which left small time for personal considerations. Ken's days were crammed with baseball and he soaked it up like a thirsty sponge. It was the happiest period of his life, marred only by the fact that it might be temporary, something too good to last. Nevertheless, he schooled himself to enjoy it while he could, gaining great satisfaction from the brand of baseball he was playing. He believed it had attained, or was approaching, big-league standards.

He studied what was going on around him. He found the Terrier veterans a close-knit group, with the sort of spirit that makes winners.

He also learned, with not too much surprise, that Beezer Crane was just about as good as he had claimed. He was a brilliant rookie hurler, with almost everything a manager could want. Despite all this, Jake Tobin wore an uncertain, speculative look at times, when his eyes rested upon Beezer Crane. Ken saw the look and knew what caused it.

Beezer was still cocky in a quiet, infuriating way and his attitude grew worse. He made no secret of his belief that fielders were of a lower order than pitchers. It was not the way to win friends or influence people, not people like the Terriers. When Beezer took the mound, there was no chattering of encouragement behind him. That was bad, a sure indication that he was riding for a fall.

Ken did his best to keep his antagonism for Cy Borg under close control, knowing his nerves could easily be affected by anger. This was no time for shaky nerves, so Ken resisted Borg's campaign to upset him.

The tension, however, was unexpectedly relieved. The relief came from sharing a common misery. It gradually developed that his roommate, Beezer Crane, had a problem somewhat similar to his own.

There were points of difference between the two problems, because in Beezer's case the element of hate was lacking. Beezer did not like Zip Regan any more than a hound dog likes a flea. He regarded Zip with a growing exasperation which could turn to sizzling anger, but which, thanks to Beezer's logic and his self-assurance, would not reach the stage of hatred.

Zip Regan was shortstop for the Terriers. He was a sophomore on the club, one year removed from the rookie ranks, and his hold upon the job was indisputable. He was a small man, not over five feet eight, and he weighed about one hundred and fifty pounds. But what he lacked in size and reach he made up for in speed. He could go with equal ease to right or left, and could jump like a kangaroo for the high ones.

His batting average seldom passed .250, but he drove opposing hurlers crazy by an uncanny ability to draw walks. He was as hard to pitch to as a midget, and as lead-off man he usually ended up on first.

He was the infield spark plug, noisy, raucous, and hard-working. He was a great help to the Terriers on the field. Off the field—well, that was a different matter, because Zip Regan had a sense of humor or what passed for one. It was seldom subtle, although it gained a slight refinement now and then through his amazing knack of imitation. He had the facile tongue of a ventriloquist in reproducing sounds or voices.

All of the Terriers, at one time or another, had felt the bludgeon of his so-called wit. There had been reprisals. They had shaved his head, tossed him in icy tubs of water, substituted shaving cream for toothpaste, but they might as well have tried to control a three-alarm fire with a water pistol.

Zip remained incorrigible, and the Terriers resigned themselves to it. Actually they might have missed his clowning. Even Tobin let him have his head, within reason, knowing the benefit of such diversions to a high-strung baseball club.

Nevertheless, the Terriers heaved a collective sigh

of relief when Zip Regan set his sights on Beezer Crane. Zip did it gleefully, because it seemed the natural thing to do. Beezer was a rookie, a definite personality, and his general appearance offered possibilities no practical joker could resist.

The first effort was mild enough. Zip entered Beezer's name in a bathing beauty contest. The committee must have felt that Beezer was a strange name for a girl, but they put it in the daily paper just the same, and the Terriers enjoyed it hugely.

So, apparently, did Beezer. He boasted of it and showed the clipping proudly, an attitude which made the joke fall flat. It also made Zip thoughtful, which was bad, for after that he really went to work on Beezer, and the Terriers gave their glad approval.

It was an interesting battle, with Zip Regan getting all the worst of it. He might as well have tried to down a hippopotamus with spitballs. All his slapstick genius struck and blunted against Beezer's calm exterior and his obvious appreciation of the jokes which often backfired against Zip. The fact was clear that Beezer Crane possessed a genius of his own.

Zip Regan's grin was not so frequent now. Occasional moodiness possessed him. He was overheard saying querulously, "The guy ain't human."

Ken Holt began to wonder, too. He restrained his curiosity for a while, then had to satisfy it. He brought the matter up one evening in the room. "How come Zip Regan doesn't get your goat?"

"He does," admitted Beezer frankly. "Like a horsefly."

"Seems more like a bumblebee to me," said Ken. "But I'm relieved to see you know what's going on."

Beezer grinned. "Old stuff," he said. "And believe it or not, Ken, I feel sort of sorry for the guy."

"Huh?" demanded Ken incredulously.

"It's like this. Zip's built himself up as a funny man and his reputation is at stake. He's cocky as a bantam rooster, with the same sort of one-track mind. He'll plug along in the same groove until he blows a gasket. That's why I'm sort of sorry for the guy. This time he's tangled with somebody out of his class."

"Superman?" asked Ken.

"Don't get me wrong," protested Beezer. "I don't mean to brag, but the point is I've been kidded by experts. My looks make me a natural stooge for guys like Zip, and I've had to learn my way around. Let the poor sucker bat his brains out. He's asked for it."

"You're darn right he has," said Ken with satisfaction. "But are you sure you can hold out?"

"A cinch, unless he finds a weak spot."

"You've got 'em?"

"Who hasn't?"

"Hum-m-m. And what if he finds one?"

"Then I'll have to slow 'im down."

"How?"

Beezer shrugged. "I'll find a way."

"He's too small for you to manhandle."

"Shucks, I know that."

Ken grinned slowly and observed, "I'd hate to have you on *my* trail."

"Thanks, son, for them kind words of understanding."

"You're welcome, pop."

Zip Regan blundered accidentally upon one of Beezer's weak spots, probably his weakest. It happened while the Terriers were traveling by bus toward a practice game with the Detroit Wolverines, who were training at Daytona.

The bus developed engine trouble ten miles short

of its destination. The driver, with appropriate remarks, got out, located the trouble, and grunted with relief.

"Not bad," he said. "Busted fan belt. I got a spare. I'll have it on in twenty minutes."

Jake Tobin said to the Terriers, "All out. Limber up."

The Terriers piled out of the bus. Tobin handed out some baseballs, and the players began tossing them back and forth on a reasonably flat space beside the road.

It was a sad excuse for a practice field, with loose sand underfoot and scrub palmetto trees reaching out to jab unwary legs with their sharp fronds. But the Terriers made the best of it. They formed two lines and began to throw.

Beezer Crane was stationed at the inside end of the line. Ken was next to him and Zip Regan was next to Ken. Zip, as usual, had to exercise his vocal cords, so he chose a haphazard subject and started. "Lots of snakes around these parts, big hungry rattlesnakes. But you guys don't have to worry while Beezer's with us, because after one look at Beezer's beak the snake'd think Beezer was a mongoose and faint dead away."

Most of the Terriers guffawed their appreciation, but this time Beezer did not join them. Glancing at him to see how he had taken it, Ken saw Beezer's muscles jerk to tautness in a quick moment of paralysis. A ball, coming at Beezer about that time, sailed past his head unnoticed. Beezer pulled himself together hurriedly, stretched his lips in a sickly grin, and started after the ball with the caution of a man upon a tightrope above Niagara Falls.

Beezer, however, did not reach the ball. It had come to rest near a small palmetto, at the base of which a rattlesnake was very busy resenting the ball's intrusion.

It was a small snake, either mentally retarded or merely showing off. It regarded the inoffensive ball with coiled ferocity, daring it to come a little closer. As part of the act, the rattler filled the air with the dry, harsh buzz of the vibrating buttons on its tail.

Beezer was fifteen feet from the snake, well out of the danger zone, when he plowed to a halt and snorted like a bee-stung horse.

His following action maintained the illusion splendidly. He snorted again, bucked high into the air, and managed somehow, while still aloft, to change direction. It was a magnificent display of exploding energy, dispelling for all time the fallacy that Beezer was lethargic.

But he hadn't even warmed up yet. He was still in low gear. He came down running, and his huge feet showed incredible ability to carry him across the sand. He scarcely lost an inch in traction, moving as if equipped with caterpillar tread.

When he reached the road, he shifted into high and really showed some speed. He headed for Daytona at a pace which, if he had held it, would have brought him in ahead of the bus schedule with lots of time to spare.

Daytona, however, was an ambitious goal even for Beezer Crane in his present earnest state of mind. Nevertheless, he held on for three hundred yards or so, which, in itself, was fancy sprinting.

He slowed down gradually and finally turned. He started toward the Terriers, who, to this point, had been too amazed to offer comment, a matter they promptly remedied when Beezer came within voice range. They let him know they had enjoyed the show tremendously. They even offered to find another snake for Beezer to outrun, complaining that he had scared the first one off.

Ken listened to them and realized something was

missing. He soon knew what it was. Zip Regan, the one man geared to make the most of such a situation, had not said a word. Ken turned worried eyes toward him and promptly knew his apprehension was well-founded. Zip Regan had a dreamy, beatific look upon his face, the expression of a man who contemplates a rosy future.

Beezer looked considerably the worse for wear when he came up. He was trying hard to regain his normal blandness, but was making little progress.

"Welcome back," Zip told him heartily. "Welcome back, my dear old pal."

A muscle twitched in Beezer's jaw. "Yeah," he said. "I thought you'd like to see me."

The driver soon announced that the bus was ready to resume its trip. Ken and Beezer sat together as they rolled along. Ken held his peace, but Beezer finally spoke. "Well, he found it."

"The weak spot?"

"Yeah. Snakes. I'm scared to death of 'em. Always have been. I know it's just plain foolishness, but every time I see one my brain freezes up and the only thing I can think of is to run. So I run. I'll bet you didn't know I was so fast. Did you?" he added with a touch of pride. "I surprise a lot of people, including myself."

"Not to mention Zip Regan."

"Ouch," said Beezer. "He'll be troublesome. He had a look in his eye—like a guy who'd just inherited a million bucks. It won't be long now."

Nor was it. The Terriers played the Wolverines that afternoon. Jake Tobin astonished everyone by sending Beezer to the mound to start the game. It was a high compliment to a rookie hurler. On the other hand, it might have been more of an experiment than a compliment. Maybe Tobin was merely testing Beezer's nerve, trying to learn if he had the self-control to pull himself together after his harrowing experience of the morning.

Beezer left no room for doubt. After a scoreless half inning for the Terriers, he ambled to the mound and began to throw his loose-jointed deliveries at the Wolverines. He set them down in order with a weak pop fly, an easy grounder to the shortstop, and a strike-out.

The Terriers pushed across a run in the top of the second. The Wolverines made no runs in the last half of the second, and Beezer came up as lead-off man in the first half of the third inning.

Beezer, to this point, had not shown much promise as a hitter, but he always tried. He ambled toward the plate, his bat dangling in his hand, and Zip Regan left the dugout almost on his heels.

There was nothing to arouse suspicion in Zip's movements, because, as head of the batting list, Zip was scheduled to be next man up. Ken, watching closely, scarcely knew what aroused his own sharp apprehension, unless it was the bland innocence of Zip Regan's manner.

Zip rested on one knee, his attention on the batter. Beezer, unaware of what was going on behind him, concentrated on the pitcher.

The first pitch, coming in too high, would obviously have been a ball, but Beezer had no way of knowing this, or caring. The ball had scarcely left the pitcher's hand when Zip played his newly acquired trick.

It was a masterpiece. The vicious rattle of a diamondback came harshly from his lips, a sound still clear and well defined in Beezer's memory.

Beezer exploded like a hand grenade, but his reaction was miraculous. Prompted by his first violent reflex, he swung his bat in a savage slash at nothing in particular. It was pure coincidence that the ball was in the way. He met it squarely, sending a terrific smash to center field. It was a line drive, too flat for a homer but powerful enough to scream across the center fielder's head and bang against the fence.

Then Beezer started running. Toward first base? Not Beezer. His first objective seemed to be the pitcher's mound. The pitcher, with a wild jump, saved himself from being trampled underfoot. Beezer did not even notice him. He steamed across the mound, passed second base with jet-propelled velocity, and took off for center field.

The center fielder, unaware of what was coming toward him, had eyes for nothing but the ball. He finally snared it, turned, and was the most astounded center fielder in the world. He was a smart player, but nothing in the books had trained him for an emergency like this.

He finally reacted in a befuddled sort of way, knowing that a runner not on base had to be tagged out with the ball. So when Beezer reached the fence and found it too tall to climb and too thick to run through, the fielder moved in to touch him with the ball in a silly apologetic manner. It was a historic moment, undoubtedly the first time in baseball annals that a base runner had been tagged out in deep center field.

The fans were in an uproar by that time, and

when Beezer made his way back to the bench he ran the gauntlet of much pointed comment. The Wolverines had plenty of delighted statements to make upon the matter, and the Terriers did not know whether to be angry or amused. Jake Tobin stood before the dugout, hands on hips, face inscrutable. Zip Regan, wearing an angelic expression, was ready to step into the batter's box.

Ken was thoughtful as he waited for his turn at bat. He had watched Beezer's performance with considerable interest, wondering what its effect would be over a long-range period. Ken hoped that a little pushing around of this sort might have a beneficial effect on Beezer's cockiness, and bring him to the understanding that there were eight men on the team beside himself. But he didn't want to see Beezer pushed around too much.

In the next two innings the Wolverines got five hits and scored three runs while Beezer was trying to pull himself together from his recent shock. He was a sober and thoughtful pitcher when Tobin finally replaced him with Lefty Piper.

The Terriers went on to win the game 4–3 with a nice rally in the eighth, and Ken Holt had the solid satisfaction of batting in the winning run with a clean single to right field. He was satisfied with his own part in the game, but considerably worried over Beezer's.

His worry was relieved by a talk with Beezer later in the evening. Beezer pulled at his long nose and said, "Maybe I'm not the fireball I had myself figured out to be."

"Maybe not," said Ken conservatively.

"They mobbed me in the fourth and fifth."

"They caught you at a bad time."

"Sure. My nerves were wobbly. But that's no excuse. A pitcher's nerves can take just as bad a licking if some guy tags him for a lucky homer. I just couldn't take it, and that's no good."

"You've got a point there," said Ken carefully, "a mighty good one. Go to work on it."

"I'm going to."

"If it pans out, you've got Zip to thank," offered Ken experimentally.

"Maybe," conceded Beezer. "But I've also got to pay him off."

"Why?"

"Just one of those things. If I do get a Terrier contract and don't get farmed out, I'll be on the same team with the little pest. He's under my hide now and he knows it. And he'll stay there until I can pin his ears back. He knows that, too."

"Any ideas?"

"Not a one. But I'll wait. I've got patience like an elephant."

5

Now that his roommate was well on the way to solving his own difficulties, Ken Holt began to realize he had some himself.

To start with, he had not received a contract yet. He believed his game was sound enough to justify a bid to join the Terriers. He wondered why Tobin didn't sign him up. Several of the other rookies had been signed. Maybe Tobin was holding off until he learned more facts about Ken's mysterious background. Maybe he wanted Ken to be more friendly with the other players, a thing which, under the circumstances, Ken couldn't bring himself to do. He could not break down the wall of reticence he had built about himself.

The hostility of Cy Borg caused another of Ken's difficulties. It occurred during a practice game.

Jake Tobin had divided the squad into two teams. They were well matched, and the game was building up to an exciting climax. Ken had played the entire game in center field, and Cy Borg had been in right field. There had been no dispute of territory until the seventh inning.

Going into the last half, Ken's team was leading 6–5. The other team got men on first and second, with one out. A good clean single would probably tie the score, and the fielders were on their toes.

Fuzz Bankhead, the Terriers' regular second baseman, strode to the plate. He was left-handed, and his hits were usually toward the first-base line. The fielders moved over to take care of this. Cy Borg was almost standing on the foul line.

The first pitch was a fireball that Bankhead seemed to like. He leaned into it, and the ball came looping in a short fly toward the outfield, taking its time as it floated through the air.

Ken noticed, however, that Bankhead had swung

a trifle late. The ball, therefore, was not hit as far to the right as usual. Instead, it came sailing into right center field.

Ken traveled at high speed toward the spot, certain he could make the catch. Normally, he reflected as he sped along, a fly ball of that sort would be taken by the right fielder, but Cy Borg would be badly handicapped for such a catch because of his position near the foul line.

Ken never knew for sure whether he or Cy Borg was at fault in the thing that happened. Ken definitely was in Borg's territory but, under the conditions, he felt he had a right to be there.

It is possible that he underestimated Borg's ability to cover ground. On the other hand, Borg may have tried for the ball in the stubborn hope of proving he was as spectacular a fielder as Ken Holt.

At any rate, *both* men tried for it. The yells of warning came too late, and they came together like a pair of charging buffalos. It was a tremendous collision. Both men hit the ground and, only by a miracle, got up uninjured.

With a bellow of wild rage Borg lunged at Ken, swinging from his knees. Ken, luckily, regained his balance soon enough to step back from the blow, and before Borg had time for another, a pair of infielders reached the scene and grabbed him.

Tobin promptly benched Cy Borg and the game continued. Both runs had scored during the mix-up in right field, and Ken's team finally lost the game.

Not that it mattered. There was too much excitement in the air, as if the Terriers were anticipating something big. It didn't take a crystal ball to tell Ken that, whatever excitement was in the wind, he was bound to be involved in it.

He was. He learned all about it when the Terriers gathered in the locker room. Tobin was there, looking grim. Borg was there with a hungry, pleased expression on his face. The Terriers were grinning with anticipation.

"Get out the gloves. Let's get this dirty business over," Tobin said.

Ken heard the words with a quick catch of satisfaction in his throat. But he was worried, too; not about himself but about the point of etiquette involved—a rookie tangling with a regular. Was this the end of things? Was this one of the more painful ways of being bounced out of big-league company?

He turned questioning eyes on Jake Tobin, who was sitting impassively on a bench. Tobin read the glance. "It's okay, kid. We're a tough outfit and proud of it. We settle our troubles in private and shake hands afterward. It helps keep the atmosphere clear. Get out the gloves, Truck."

A quick surge of elation rushed through Ken's veins. It was caused not so much by the permission to stage the fight as by the manner in which Tobin had granted that permission.

Ken believed that Tobin would not take the risk of letting one of his star players fight a rookie unless it were reasonably certain that the rookie was headed for a position on the team. A contract with the Terriers! That, in itself, would be worth a dozen lickings.

Not that Ken Holt intended taking a licking. He had been reared in a rough school. Brawls were no novelty to him. He had had to fight to exist, and he wouldn't have existed long if he had not known how to use his fists. He yanked off his spiked shoes with fierce anticipation.

Truck Hawley produced two pairs of ten-ounce gloves. Ken noted they were well worn. He would have preferred bare fists, but he saw the wisdom of this precaution. A player's hands are valuable. He stuck out his own to receive the gloves.

A space of some twenty feet was left after the Terriers had formed a circle. Ken moved into this space and faced the larger man.

"We don't have any rounds here, Holt," announced Tobin from his seat upon the bench. "Just fight clean. All right, men, get goin'!"

Borg needed no further invitation. He came in with a rush, swinging his big arms. That was his first mistake. It was a careless attack. Ken side-stepped the rush, throwing a straight left as he did so. It smacked solidly against the exposed side of Cy Borg's head.

Borg didn't like it. He came in again, grunting with anger, and swinging from all points of the compass. Ken did not entirely escape that barrage of blows. One of them caught him high on the forehead, and he felt the bruising power behind the other's fists.

Ken managed, however, to slow Borg down with another left. He also crossed a right. It was a nice punch. It connected cleanly just in front of Borg's ear, and Ken got the uneasy impression that Borg's head was about as vulnerable as a bowling ball.

Borg, having the advantage of weight and strength, forced the fighting. He did not depend on science, but he had the power and vitality of a grizzly bear. Every punch he threw was dangerous.

Ken was forced to take the defensive, but his skill, luckily, was greater than that of Borg. It kept him from being hammered to a pulp, although it did not save him from punishment.

Borg's intention seemed to be to end the battle with all possible speed, which was just the thing Ken wanted to avoid. He was fighting for time, trying to conserve his strength until Borg's power began to wane.

Borg finally realized this and used an old trick. His attack slowed. His arms seemed heavy. A look of frustration appeared upon his face. Ken, thinking this was the moment he had waited for, moved swiftly in. Borg came to life and caught him with a vicious, looping right.

The blow, fortunately, was high on the head. Ken hit the floor, but his brains, though addled, remained working. It even occurred to him that Borg might fall for the same trick himself.

Ken came up on one knee. He shook his head, pretending to be in worse shape than he really was. Finally he staggered to his feet, and Borg, with a snort of triumph, came rushing in for the kill.

It was Ken's cue and he played it smartly. As Borg charged at him, Ken's legs snapped back to life and he went in under Borg's guard like a panther.

Two short driving blows caught Borg in the mid-section. The breath squealed out of him. He had sense enough to cover up, however, gaining time to catch his breath. Ken stepped back, grateful for the moment's rest he so badly needed.

Cy Borg recovered quickly and came back to the attack. This time his steam was definitely at lower pressure. Four minutes of high-speed fighting, plus two hard blows, would slow down anyone not trained for it.

Borg had definitely slowed down, while Ken had managed to keep something in reserve. Not much, but enough if Ken kept his head. Assured of this, he slipped inside of Cy Borg's next swing. He sank another blow just below the wishbone, and when Cy Borg doubled up Ken caught him with a wicked uppercut.

It did not floor the big man. Punch-drunk and dazed, he came pawing in again, wide open and ready to be chopped to pieces. Ken feinted at Borg's middle once again. Borg dropped his guard to protect that vulnerable spot. His jaw loomed up, and Ken, at the risk of a broken hand, threw a knockout punch.

It was a bull's-eye. Borg stood there, glassy-eyed. As he started to topple, Ken stepped in and caught him, saving him from a nasty fall.

It was a clean-cut victory, but there were neither congratulations nor condolences. It was the law of the Brickyard Gang that these things should be taken in their stride. Only one formality remained.

Borg came around fast. He was sitting sullenly on a bench when Jake Tobin grabbed Ken's arm and shoved him silently in Borg's direction. Ken knew what Tobin meant, but he didn't know whether or not he was supposed to say anything. So he merely stuck out his hand.

Borg accepted it with obvious repugnance. The gesture fulfilled the contract of the law, but no one could doubt, least of all Ken Holt, that the spirit was sadly lacking. Borg's eyes were venomous as they flitted for an instant across his.

6

Things were outwardly peaceful between Ken and Borg in the days that followed, tense, driving days wherein Jake Tobin tried to put the finishing touches on the Terriers before exhibiting them to their rabid fans in Philadelphia.

Ken settled himself comfortably in the groove, but Beezer Crane experienced tougher going. Zip Regan had him where he wanted him, and he made the most of it.

It was significant, however, that Zip restrained himself from giving rattlesnake imitations on the baseball field. It seemed obvious enough that Jake

Tobin was behind this good behavior, a fact which galled the pride of Beezer Crane.

"I don't need help against that dizzy little shortstop," he protested gloomily to Ken.

It was an optimistic statement, as events soon proved. Beezer staged several spectacular stampedes under the stimulus of Zip's imitative talent. One of the demonstrations took place in the dining room, on which occasion Beezer failed to notice a couple of tables that happened to be in his way. It was quite a mess, forcing Beezer to admit to Ken, "I gotta take this thing in hand."

He did so—in heroic fashion. Ken noted his absence on successive mornings, and noted his pale, strained look when he returned. Ken restrained his curiosity carefully, knowing Beezer would talk when he was ready.

He was ready after the third time he returned without the pale, strained look. "I've licked it," he said grimly.

"How?" asked Ken.

"I've been visiting a rattlesnake farm where they raise rattlers for their poison, skins, and"—he shuddered only slightly—"for food. They put 'em in cans like salmon."

"You must have had a lot of fun," said Ken.

"Hilarious," said Beezer. "But it did the trick. The owner of the farm was a swell guy. He used to be scared of snakes himself, so he helped me over the bumps. I heard so many of 'em rattle I can take it in my stride."

Which turned out to be true. Zip's best efforts from then on fell flat. He soon gave up this aspect of the struggle, but was not discouraged. His energy remained unflagging, with Beezer as the target, but the battle was now back on even terms.

In a bigger fight than that, however, Beezer triumphed. The attitude of the Terriers toward him was gradually changing for the better. He worked hard, put aside his cockiness, and tried to learn the things the veterans could teach him. The result was that he became a better pitcher, steadier and more cooperative.

Ken was alone in the room one evening toward the end of the training season. He was reading a magazine, but he forgot the story when Beezer burst into the room, his mouth stretched in a wide grin.

"I got it, Ken!" he yelped. "I'm in! Tobin just signed me up. He's not even farming me out. I'm going north with the Terriers."

Ken jumped from the chair and grabbed his

roommate's hand. "Nice goin', guy," he said. "Great stuff!"

"You're next," said Beezer promptly, before Ken had a chance to feel a surge of envy. "Jake's waiting in his office for you now. He told me to send you up."

Ken felt a surge of exultation, but it died as swiftly as it came. He didn't know quite why, but the sudden high excitement was replaced by a cold chill down his spine. For the past few weeks he had been virtually certain of his contract. But now, with the big moment right on top of him, he wasn't sure. There was the matter of his hidden background. Would Tobin overlook it?

Some of the color must have drained from Ken Holt's face. Beezer stared at him, then said with gruff exasperation, "Cut it out! Don't be an imbecile. You've got the job sewed up."

Ken swallowed hard and managed a weak grin. "I hope you're right. But I'll never find out by standing here and guessing. Here goes, pal. Keep your fingers crossed."

He left the room and started for Tobin's office, two floors above. He used the stairs, rather than the elevator, trying to gain time to pull himself together. He had managed it to some extent by the time he reached the door. He stiffened the muscles of his face and knocked.

"Come in!" yelled Tobin from the other side.

Ken's palm was slippery on the knob. He opened the door and entered the room. Jake Tobin was sitting at a desk and on top of it lay several legal-looking documents. Ken knew what they were and felt a new tightness in his throat.

He studied Tobin's face as he crossed the room, hoping for some sign of the manager's intentions. Nothing showed. The face was blank. Tobin motioned to a chair beside the desk and said, "Sit down, Ken."

Ken eased himself into a chair. Tobin toyed with a fountain pen and kept his eyes on it. Without looking up, he said, "Still want to be a man of mystery, Ken?"

Ken's breath jammed in his throat. He sensed an ultimatum in Jake Tobin's words but couldn't be quite sure. He took a careful breath and said, "I'd prefer it that way."

Tobin shrugged. Ken had the panicky feeling that Tobin was about to drop the ax but was giving Ken a last-minute chance to prevent the execution.

Ken's eyes fastened hungrily on the legal document near Tobin's hand. It was undoubtedly his contract, the lever Tobin would try to use to pry into Ken's past. And Ken knew it was an effective lever. He began sweating as he struggled to face the revelation of his secret.

But Tobin fooled him. Raising his eyes to catch the direction of Ken's stare, he said, "Yeah, Ken. It's your contract." He reached for the paper and flipped it toward Ken. "Read it and sign it, if it suits you."

Ken's hand went impulsively toward the contract, then froze in midair, held there by a restraining force he could not analyze at once.

Tobin, however, seemed to understand it. "No strings attached," he said. "It's yours."

"But—but—"

"Yeah, I know. You believed I'd insist on knowing something about your background first. I'd like to know," he admitted frankly, "but I'm banking on my judgment. I'm assuming that whatever you're keeping to yourself will not harm the Terriers when it becomes known—as it is bound to."

Ken thought this over carefully for several moments. His eyes met Tobin's steadily when he finally said, "You have my word that, to the best of my belief, the Terriers will not be harmed in any way."

Tobin nodded his acceptance, then said thoughtfully, "There's another angle you may have overlooked—the newspapers. If you show as much stuff in our regular games as you've shown in training camp, the sport scribes will be after you like bloodhounds."

"It's a chance I'll have to take."

"Maybe I can make the chance a little easier," said Tobin. Then he added irritably, "Although I don't know why I should, except that it'll be fun to slip over a little reverse English on the sport writers." He grinned with slow relish. "I think I know now what makes 'em tick. I ought to know. I've tangled with 'em enough times." He pulled out a cigar and lighted it, while Ken waited curiously. When Tobin had a light that suited him, he grinned again. "I'm a publicity hound so far as my team is concerned. It pays off in the gate receipts to keep the Terriers colorful. Maybe I've pulled a few fast ones on the scribes. They seem to think so, and are out to pay me back—in a nice way, you understand. Or do you?"

"No," said Ken, "I don't."

"No reason why you should," said Tobin reasonably. "It's this way. They think I've hollered 'Wolf!' too often. I'll really holler about you, by which I mean I'll build the mystery angle up as corny as an ear of Golden Bantam. I'll . . . now let me think . . . yes, I'll bill you as the Fielder from Nowhere. That ought to get 'em."

"Maybe," said Ken doubtfully, still wondering what it was all about.

Tobin laughed. "Just leave it to me, son. Now sign the contract, if it suits you."

Ken read it briefly, then signed his name with a hand not entirely steady.

Jake Tobin said, "That's that. Now beat it. I've got work to do."

Returning to his room, Ken broke the news to Beezer. Beezer let out a glad bellow and pounded Ken upon the back. Ken turned and snapped a playful punch to Beezer's ribs. Both men were feeling great.

7

The Terriers broke camp and headed north, stopping along the way for several practice games. They were playing well, despite the usual ragged edges that would be smoothed out later in the season.

A few sport scribes offered the cautious prediction that foxy Jake Tobin was bringing a probable pennant-snatcher into the race. They pointed out departments in which the team was stronger than ever before, and in doing this they did not overlook Ken Holt.

In fact, the name of Holt found a prominent place

in early copy. He was one of those natural rookies sport writers pray for. When things were dull and they had to meet a deadline, they could always write a column on a rookie like Ken Holt.

The proceeded to do so, until Duke Gallup, one of the oldest and smartest of the writers, bethought himself of the past. "Who is this flashy youngster, Holt?" he asked in his daily column. "Where does he hail from and where did he learn that brand of baseball?

"I'll admit that we gentlemen of the press would like to know but, on the other hand, this begins to take on the unmistakable aroma of another of Jake Tobin's parlor tricks. Holt isn't the first rookie he's pulled out of a hat when he really needed one.

"But why the mystery? Why the spectacular buildup of letting the boy wander into training camp like a hobo? It would almost seem that Jake is working a little too hard to stir up publicity for the Terriers. You wouldn't be trying to pull another fast one on us gullible newspaper reporters and sport fans, would you, Jake?"

This article by Duke Gallup struck a note that warned off the other baseball experts. It was only too true that the astute Jake Tobin had tricked them into valuable publicity in other instances, and even though they all liked Tobin, they didn't want to be taken in again.

So they toned down the mystery angle and treated Ken Holt merely as another promising rookie. If they still wondered where he came from, they didn't say so in their stories. Nor did they ask either Tobin or Ken for the information. They did not want to give Tobin that much satisfaction.

Ken Holt was grateful. He was also impressed by Tobin's shrewdness in the matter. Ken was not courting the sort of publicity that would encourage people to delve into his past. He was a baseball player now, and he wanted to remain one.

The Brickyard Gang had accepted him as a member of the team by the time the season opened, but they found him wary of close friendships with anyone but Beezer Crane. Ken wanted to make other friendships, but he didn't dare. Not for a while, at any rate.

Ken was accepted as a member of the team, but not as one of the Terriers themselves. There was a difference. They took him for granted as a baseball player, and a good one, but they respected the barrier Ken had raised and didn't try to cross it.

The relationship between the Terriers and Ken was exemplified, undeliberately but clearly, by Zip Regan, whose delight in slapstick comedy remained unchecked. No joke was too insignificant for Zip to play, and no member of the club was safe from him. No member, that is, but Ken Holt.

Ken tried to consider himself lucky in this respect. But there were times when he had the wish that Zip would try to pull a fast one on him. Zip, however, aimed his shafts at other targets, ignoring Ken in a pointed way that told Ken where he stood.

When the Terriers stopped over for a practice game in Baltimore, Zip turned his attention to Joe Flynn, a notoriously heavy sleeper who bragged that he could sleep in a boiler foundry. Zip, being a searcher after truth, decided to prove Flynn's statement and persuaded some of the others to lend a hand.

There was a department store across the street from the hotel in which the Terriers were staying, and one of the show windows displayed a set of bedroom furniture. The night watchman of the store succumbed to a heavy bribe, and the stage was set.

Joe Flynn turned out to be as heavy a sleeper as

he had claimed to be. Late at night six Terriers carried the spring mattress, with Flynn still on it, out of the hotel room, down the freight elevator, out a side door of the hotel, and across the deserted street to the department store. A short time later Flynn was slumbering peacefully in his new bed, right in the middle of the show window.

All of the Terriers, with the exception of Ken Holt, were awakened in time to see the climax of the act. Ken got the story, secondhand, from Beezer Crane, and it was obvious that he had missed something quite worthwhile.

Joe Flynn, it appeared, had a sizable audience, in addition to the Terriers, when he awakened. The sidewalk was packed with appreciative watchers when Flynn climbed out of bed and, groggy with sleep, stood dazedly in his pajamas trying to figure where he was. When he finally got it figured out, he suffered a moment of shocked paralysis, then dove for the bed. The bed collapsed beneath his weight, but Flynn remained huddled under the covers until rescued by angry employees of the department store. They drew the curtains across the wide window, provided Flynn with temporary clothes, and got him out of there.

Beezer related the incident between spasms of laughter. When he had finished, he calmed down enough to say, "I think Zip overstepped himself this time. There'll be trouble. And I hope the little wise guy gets it in the neck."

There was trouble, quite a lot of it. The executives of the department store were not easy to appease. It required all of the Terriers' prestige to do so, and Jake Tobin was a very furious baseball manager. He slapped a two hundred dollar fine on Regan and a hundred dollars on each man who helped him.

"I think," said Beezer later, "Tobin let Zip off too easy. The guy's a little cracked when it comes to comedy. The fellows on the team play along with him now, but if they ever get fed up with his monkeyshines, which they will, I'd hate to be the manager of the Terriers."

Ken agreed with Beezer's prophecy but did not give it much more thought. He had something more important on his mind—the baseball of Ken Holt. He understood the tremendous importance of making a good showing in his first appearance before the Terrier fans.

The Terriers opened the season on their home grounds against the Chicago Rangers, who, the year before, had come within a whisker of winning the League flag. They were as strong as ever, a dangerous team.

Moreover, they were well aware of one of the strong superstitions of the Terrier camp. The Terriers, to the last man, were convinced the opening game was probably the most important one of the entire schedule. Win that game, the story went, and they couldn't fail to finish in the first division. Lose it, and they would surely end in the lower brackets.

Up to the present it had almost invariably worked out that way, and the Terriers were thoroughly convinced of the infallibility of the rule. They also knew that the Rangers would like nothing better than to defeat them in the opening game.

The Terriers cherished another equally strong fantasy. This, too, was the result of sheer coincidence, but just try to tell that to a bunch of superstitious ballplayers. On the last three occasions when the Terriers had lost the opener and had finished in the second division, the decisive element in the defeat had been a rookie. Therefore the Terriers were violently opposed to starting a rookie in the opening game.

Because of this, things came to a rather serious

head in the locker room before the game. A committee headed by Cy Borg brought its protest to Jake Tobin. "You know how it is, Jake," said Borg doggedly. "It'll be suicide to start Holt. It takes only one rookie to lose a game."

The approach turned out to be a tactical blunder. Tobin might or might not have started Holt, but he did not like to have his players tell him what to do. Furthermore, he had fought a bitter campaign for years in an effort to shatter the Terriers' first-game superstition. His face got red.

"Listen!" he roared. "Is this a baseball club or a tribe of voodoo worshipers? Have you birds got any brains of your own, or do you pull all of your bright ideas out of a mumbo-jumbo jug? Now get out on the diamond and pretend you're grown-up. Ken Holt starts in center field!"

Ken heard all this, and a shiver traveled up his spine. This was one game during which he would have liked to stay right on the bench. Not that he doubted his own ability. It was merely that baseball was a funny and unpredictable game.

He wanted desperately to get off on the right foot with the fans and with his teammates. It might mean success or failure with the Terriers. Plenty of players had been sent to the minors under the pressure of team and fan antagonism, and just one little accident out there today might do the trick. It was not a pleasant outlook.

So Ken Holt went into his first major-league game with an unnatural tenseness. He was as nervous as a cat. He even found himself hoping that no balls would come his way.

None did in the top of the first inning, but they went almost everywhere else on the field. Before Lefty Piper could settle down, the Rangers rammed out a couple of short singles to put men on first and second with no one out.

The third Ranger laid down a nice sacrifice bunt along the first-base line, advancing his teammates to second and third with one out. The fourth man hammered a vicious grounder to Zip Regan at short. The best Zip could do was to knock it down. He recovered fast and whipped it to the plate, too late by the flicker of an eyelash. The runner slid in safe, leaving men on first and third.

The next Ranger doubled to left field. A second run scored, leaving men on second and third. Herb Green, another Terrier pitcher, was warming up hurriedly in the bullpen.

But Lefty Piper had plenty of nerve left. He showed it now by blazing a pair of strikes in quick succession past the batter. The Ranger fouled off the next one to the screen and then went down swinging at a wicked hook.

The Terriers finally retired the side when the next Ranger lifted a long, lazy fly to left field, where Hap Cross gobbled it up after a short run.

The Terriers, trailing by two runs, came in for their turn at bat. They tried to show confidence, but Ken was aware of the gloomy glances shot in his direction. Incredible as it seemed, the Terriers appeared to be blaming him for the Rangers' two-run lead. They already had decided he was a jinx.

Cy Borg summed up the situation. "Well, what'd you expect?" he asked with a resigned shrug of his big shoulders.

Tobin gave him a fierce glance. "Shut up!" he snapped. Then he said acidly to the rest of the team in general, "Now remember, boys, somebody's put the evil eye on you. That isn't a resin bag you see out there on the mound. Those are the ground-up bones of a cross-eyed skunk, killed in a graveyard at the dark of the moon. Whenever a Ranger touches that bag, it means that no batter can hit anything he throws. So you see, my bright young crystal-gazers, he's got you licked. Now let's see how fast you can get up there and strike out."

None of the scowling Terriers seemed to think there was anything very funny about Jake's speech. Zip Regan, lead-off man, was muttering to himself as he strode to the plate and settled himself in the batter's box.

Sure enough, the Ranger's southpaw, Slim Tucker, dusted his fingers with the resin bag before the first delivery. Zip got a toehold and waved his bat in challenge. Tucker went into a limber windup, and the ball came streaking toward the plate.

It was a fireball slightly off dead center. Zip took a jerky swing at it, and, either by luck or accident, connected with a clean single over second. Ken breathed easier, hoping that a solid hit on the first ball pitched might shake the Terriers from their jitters.

Joe Flynn, first baseman, came to the plate with a determined air. The best he could do was to lob a high foul over toward the dugout behind first base. The Ranger first baseman, hustling, made the catch.

Hap Cross, left fielder, did not go far toward helping the Terrier cause. He worked the count to three and two and then went out on a called third strike.

Cy Borg, the cleanup man, went to the plate with his black war club. He was always a dangerous hitter, and Ken Holt was tortured by the possibilities involved if Borg rapped out a single or, even worse, a skimpy double that would leave Terriers on second and third. This would saddle Ken with the responsibility of bringing both men in.

Borg, however, saved him any further concern in the matter by hitting the first ball pitched on a long fly into center field. The center fielder caught it after a long run, retiring the side.

Ken headed for his center field position, well aware of the apprehensive glances of his teammates. There was nothing really personal in these glances. They merely regarded him as they might have regarded a bug in their breakfast food.

Lefty Piper began to get the range in the second inning. One batter got a weak scratch single, but he disposed of the next three quite handily.

Then Ken Holt came to the plate to lead off for the Brickyard Gang in their half of the inning. He wanted a hit desperately at that moment. He wanted to give these crazy teammates of his a little confidence. He wanted to hammer the idea into their heads that he was an asset rather than a liability.

The idea was a fine one, if Slim Tucker would cooperate. His first hook, however, broke with accurate speed. Ken missed the ball by a good six inches, developing, at the same time, a healthy respect for the lanky hurler on the mound.

Tucker felt him out with a couple of wide ones, but Ken ignored them. He slashed hard at the fourth delivery and fouled it on the ground behind third base. The next ball was a little close. Ken let it go, and the count was three and two.

Ken concentrated on the next pitch with everything he had, but he did not concentrate enough. Tucker used his floater for the first time that day, a beautifully deceptive ball. Tucker looked as if he were throwing a fastball, yet it came sailing up to the plate like a toy balloon.

Ken had started his swing before he realized Tucker had tricked him. The result was very sad indeed. He swung himself half off his feet, and the ball plopped gently into the catcher's mitt. The crowd laughed.

"Give 'im a tennis racket!" someone bawled.

It was not an easy job to walk back to the Terrier dugout. It seemed to Ken that he almost had to force his way against the hard stares coming out to meet him, a melancholy beginning for a young fellow in the big leagues. It was small consolation to watch the other Terriers go down in order.

8

In the top of the third, Lefty Piper looked as if he had really settled down. He polished off the first Ranger with a third called strike. The second batter lifted a high foul behind the plate. Hawley flipped off his mask, sprinted back toward the screen, and made the catch. The third Ranger trickled a weak grounder back to Piper, who scooped it up and tossed it to Joe Flynn at first. The Rangers went down in order.

In the last of the third, the Terriers showed signs of life. Hal Mercer, their peppery third baseman, hit a single over the shortstop's head on the first pitch.

Lefty Piper came to the plate. He was a poor hitter, so Tobin decided that he stood a better chance of laying down a bunt than of getting a base hit.

Lefty went after the first pitch, shoving it along the first-base line. The bunt was too hard. The Ranger first baseman came in fast, fielded the ball with his bare hand, and decided he had a play at second for a forceout. He made the throw but it was wide, pulling the second baseman off the bag. Mercer slid in safely. Lefty Piper, looking surprised and pleased, reached first.

The top of the Terrier list came up to bat. Zip Regan strutted to the plate and waved his war club at the pitcher. He took a ball and a called strike, then nudged another bunt down the first-base line. It was a perfect sacrifice, permitting no play except at first base. Zip, of course, was out, but Mercer and Piper had advanced to third and second, and were now in a position to tie the score if either of the next Terriers could get a hit.

Joe Flynn failed to get a hit, but he got the next best thing to it—a long fly ball to deep center. Mercer tagged up at third and scored easily after the catch. The throw from center field came to third base, holding Piper on second.

Hap Cross did his best to bring Piper in with the tying run, but his looping fly to right was caught by the Ranger right fielder for the final out.

As Ken headed for his center field position at the start of the fourth, he was still fighting against nervous tension. What, he wondered, would happen if he got a hard fielding chance? Would he handle it or would he get a bad case of buck fever and misjudge it?

It wasn't a pleasant possibility to contemplate, and he hated himself for permitting such thoughts to gallop through his mind. He had never doubted himself to this extent before. But then, never before had he found himself in such a vitally important baseball game. The palms of his hands were slippery with perspiration. He was wiping the palm of his right hand on his pants when the first Ranger batter lifted a fly to center field.

Ken saw the ball come arching toward him. His first urge was to burst into some sort of frantic action, but a violent spasm of his nerves held him rooted to the spot. At least it seemed that way to Ken. Probably his inability to move was nothing more than baseball instinct. As it was, he did not have to move more than a few short steps to his left. He was scarcely aware that the ball had settled cozily in his glove.

Once he felt it there, he was tremendously relieved and grateful, grateful that the chance had been an easy one, the sort he normally could have caught in his hip pocket. He was grateful for the smooth feel of the horsehide in his hand. He held it an instant longer, feeling his confidence flow back. When he finally threw it toward the infield he was grinning, surprised that he had ever allowed himself to doubt. He heard the sardonic, loud applause of Terrier fans, but he didn't care.

He was even hoping for a harder chance. He had recovered from his fielding jitters and was ready for bigger things.

The second Ranger to face Piper hit the third pitch for a double off the left field wall. Piper tightened up. He struck the next man out, but got a little careless with the fourth, the Ranger's husky catcher, Trask. Piper tried to hook the outside corner on a three-two pitch, but the curve did not break in time and the ball came in right over the center of the plate.

Big Trask connected with it squarely. Ken saw

the ball flash off the bat. He saw it head for center field. He waited a fleeting instant to judge the ball's trajectory. He knew that Trask's wallop was a mighty one but that he had a chance to make the catch.

Ken Holt had speed, a lot of it, and he knew he would need it now. Running high upon his toes, he headed for the wall. The blurred features of the bleacher fans were spread above it.

He reached the concrete wall and whirled, his back against it, and caught the quick flash of the ball, a trifle to his left. He made two lightning steps, and still had time to leap into the air.

He felt the ball slug hard into his mitt, banging his gloved hand back against cement. The impact jarred the ball from the pocket of his glove. It tumbled toward the ground, but Ken's right hand swooped through to grab it near his waist. This time he held it.

The rowdy bleacherites approved of the catch and they roared appreciation. One leather-lung blared out, "Nice goin', Holt! Maybe you're good enough for us, after all! Let's see you get a hit!"

It was warm praise in a left-handed sort of way, but Ken was smart enough to catch the qualifying element, even the mild threat, implied. They were willing to admit he was a fielder. But could he bat? Fielding was all right in its place, but the only sure way to a fan's heart was to hit the ball into the stands.

Ken's catch had saved a run, and the Terriers were fair enough to show their gratitude when he came to the dugout. It was a pleasant moment. However, Ken still had to prove he knew what a baseball bat was for, and he would have his second chance this inning. He forced his thoughts away from everything but batting.

Cy Borg led off for the Terriers in the bottom of the fourth. The fans howled loudly for a hit, and Borg came close to giving them one. He blasted a line drive over first, but the Ranger first baseman made a circus catch, and Borg, halfway down the path, pulled up, shook his head disgustedly, and headed for the bench.

Ken came to bat again. He was steady and relaxed this time. He had studied Tucker's work attentively, and felt no further awe of him, an attitude that showed in the concise economy of his movements as he settled himself in the batter's box.

Slim Tucker was not stupid. He caught the change

of attitude and paid Ken Holt the compliment of regarding him respectfully. He offered Ken a low hook on the first delivery. Ken let it go. Tucker blazed in a fastball for the second try. It was a trifle close, but Ken liked the looks of it and swung.

He connected squarely, but knew he had swung too soon. He pulled a tremendous foul into the second deck of the left field grandstand. It went for nothing but a strike, but was the type of authoritative blow that makes a pitcher extremely nervous.

Tucker took time out to dust his fingers on the resin bag. He stepped to the mound, nodded agreement to the catcher's sign, and went to work again. Ken took a low delivery for another ball. He swung at the fourth offering and lined another hard foul behind third base, a grounder this time. Then he changed his stance a trifle to compensate, if possible, for the fact that he was swinging early.

Seeing what was going on, Tucker tried to lure Ken into a swing by giving him a wide one. Ken let it go for the third ball, and the count was full.

Tucker set himself carefully for the pay-ball. He blazed it in, trying to hook it across the plate from the outside corner. But he did not pull it off. The ball came in too low and hooked too late. Regretfully, Ken let it go. He had wanted to get a hit, but a free trip to first base was not to be despised.

As he jogged along the white line, he hoped the fans were reasonably satisfied. Naturally they would have preferred to see him get a hit, but they must know that it took some ability to work a pitcher like Slim Tucker for a walk. Jake Tobin, coaching at first base, seemed pleased.

"Nice goin', Ken," he said.

Fuzz Bankhead came to bat, and Ken caught Tobin's almost imperceptible sign as he signaled Bankhead to sacrifice Ken to second base. Ken waited to be sure that Tucker's throw was not a pitchout, then set sail for second base.

He heard Jake Tobin's yell of warning just in time. Ken plowed to a halt, caught a quick glimpse of what had happened, then dug in hard to get back to first.

Bankhead, in attempting to bunt, had popped a high ball to the pitcher. Fortunately it was high enough to allow Ken to get back in time—but only just.

With two out, Tobin signaled Ken to steal. Ken's heart took a quick jump of excitement, then settled down. It was logical enough for him to steal just now, and the Rangers knew it. If he could reach second base, a hit could bring him in to tie the score.

Tucker tried a couple of fast pickoffs at first base, but Ken, despite his big lead, slid in both times under the tag. From then on it was a guessing game, and Ken knew Tobin would do the guessing for the Terriers, a matter promptly taken care of when Tucker went into a fast windup.

"No!" snapped Tobin.

Ken held first base and, sure enough, Tobin had guessed right. Tucker sent a pitchout past the batter, Hawley. The Ranger catcher was all set for the throw to second, and Ken probably would have been out had he attempted to steal.

Tucker tried another pickoff. Ken hit the ground and came in safely on his belly. Dust gritted in his teeth, but he scarcely noticed it. On the next pitch Tobin sent him off with a sharp, "Go!"

Ken exploded into action like a sprinter. Second base seemed miles away. He saw the second baseman, Carter, crouching to receive the throw. He also saw that Carter's legs were scientifically placed, his left foot planted toward first base and slightly back, a position that would effectively block any attempt at a deceptive hook slide to the rear of the bag.

So when Ken hit the dirt, feet first, he hurtled directly at the bag. He went in under Carter like a thunderbolt. He heard the slap of the ball in Carter's glove, but when Carter banged the ball against his leg, Ken's feet were already against the sack. He was certain he was safe, but confirmed it by an upward glance through the cloud of dust. Sure enough, the umpire had his palms out parallel to the ground.

Ken climbed to his feet and dusted off. He was pleased with his performance, more pleased than ever when he heard the fans yell their approval. Maybe they were finally recognizing the fact that Ken Holt was a ball player. It was about time they found it out, Ken told himself, beginning to feel a little cocky.

His feeling of self-assurance was not lessened when Truck Hawley got a solid single to left center field. Ken crossed the plate with the tying run, not forgetting that he could not have scored the run if he had not stolen second base. He hoped the Terrier fans would not forget it either. Hal Mercer grounded out to short to retire the side, but the Terriers were back in the ball game with a 2–2 score.

In the top of the fifth, Lefty Piper set the Rangers

down in order. In the bottom of the fifth, the Terriers got a man as far as second, but no farther.

Both teams threatened in the sixth and seventh innings, but neither could get a man across the plate to break the deadlock. Ken had another batting chance in the sixth. With a man on first he sent a long fly to center field. It was a nice try, but the center fielder pulled it down and Ken Holt was still without a hit.

When the Rangers came up to bat to start the eighth, they showed a firm intention to get down to work and break the tie. Their dugout shouted encouragement as the first man strode to the plate. He promptly dropped a Texas leaguer out behind the shortstop.

The next man sacrificed him to second. Then Lefty Piper bore down hard to retire the third man, swinging. The fourth man up was a portside hitter, and the fielders shifted to the right.

The Ranger took two balls and a called strike, then connected with the fourth delivery. It was a long-hit fly to right center field, and it promised to land somewhere between Borg and Ken. Both men sprinted for the spot.

Ken had perhaps the best claim on the ball, although he was not too sure of it at the time. It presented a reasonably easy chance for a running catch.

As he ran Ken's mind was as active as his legs. His suspicions of Cy Borg had never been entirely stilled. He felt that the man would go to almost any extreme to satisfy a personal grudge, and the present moment was a perfect opportunity.

Borg had the upper hand because, as a veteran, he was supposed to call all close catches where a difference of opinion might arise. His word was law, a fact that had been drilled into Ken by Tobin.

As he raced along, Ken was almost certain Borg would never let him make the catch, even though Ken might have the advantage of position. And so firmly was this conviction fixed in his mind that Borg's words hit him with an almost physical force.

"Take it, Holt!" snapped Borg.

It was the last thing Ken had expected, and he felt a quick premonition of treachery. He was completely ruled at that instant by suspicion, and this raised havoc with his coordination.

It should have been an easy out. Borg stopped in plenty of time to give him a free hand. But Ken muffed the catch. It hit the fingers of his glove and bounced into the clear.

In the following swift action, Cy Borg recovered

the ball. The Ranger runner had started from second at the crack of the bat and was already across the plate with the run that broke the tie. Borg made the throw to second, but the runner slid in under it.

It was an ugly moment for Ken Holt. He wanted to find a nice deep hole and crawl to the bottom of it. He had allowed his stupid fears to make a fool of him. Borg had not tried to double-cross him after all. He had called the play as fairly as he could. Ken expected an outburst from him, but the big right fielder flicked just one contemptuous glance in Ken's direction.

The next Ranger grounded out to first, but the damage was already done. The rookie jinx was riding high again. Ken was all prepared to be taken out of the game, but Jake Tobin, for some dogged reason of his own, refused to send him to the showers. Ken sat miserably on the bench while the Terriers tried to start a rally. But the rally faded out with two weak hits. No runners crossed the plate. The score was still 3–2.

The visitors made no runs in the ninth, and took the field for the last half, grimly determined to protect the precious one-run gift from Ken.

The top of the Terrier list was up, which was

something in their favor. Zip Regan led off with his second hit of the day, a sharp single over first. Joe Flynn sacrificed Zip to second. Then Hap Cross drew one of the few walks Tucker had given that afternoon. The Terrier fans came to life, roaring for a score.

Cy Borg did his best. He lined a deep grounder behind first base. The first baseman made a brilliant stop which left him too far off balance to attempt a double play. So he flipped the ball to Tucker, who was covering at first. Borg went out, and Regan ended up on third, with Cross on second.

There was no yelling now among the Terrier fans as the rookie, Ken Holt, headed for the plate. He was greeted by a stony, disapproving silence, shortly broken by a raucous voice. "Give us a pinch hitter!"

It struck a note of popular appeal, and soon the fans were howling like a pack of wolves, demanding that Tobin break the jinx by leaving Ken upon the bench.

Ken half expected Tobin to accede to the demand, to change his mind at the last minute and relieve him of the tremendous load that had been dumped upon his shoulders. Ken even had the feeling that Tobin was sending him to the plate out of sheer stubbornness, a bullheaded intention of proving he was boss, that he could not be moved by pressure from fans or players.

Then in a clear flash of intuition Ken knew this wasn't so. He knew, beyond a doubt, that no amount of stubbornness would move Jake Tobin to an act he didn't believe in. Nothing would sway the soundness of his judgment so far as the welfare of the Terriers was concerned. The Terriers came first with him, and all his shrewdness and experience would be utilized to help them win.

It brought the present situation to a sharper focus for Ken Holt. Tobin's decision to let him go to bat could have but one significance—Jake was convinced that Ken was the best man for the job. Otherwise a pinch hitter would be heading for the plate right now.

The moment of swift understanding bolstered Ken's wavering confidence and gave him the fresh assurance he so badly needed. Best of all, it aided him to build a wall about himself, a tough protective shell from which the yelling of the fans bounced back like small shot from armor plate. It helped him to limit his entire world to the small confines of the baseball diamond, and to limit the people in the world to the Ranger hurler and himself.

Slim Tucker also understood the importance of the next few moments. Only a single batter, Ken Holt, stood between him and victory. The pitcher stepped unhurriedly upon the mound, studied Ken carefully, got his sign, and went into a full windup.

A fireball came in, shooting sparks. It looked a trifle wide to Ken, so he let it go. The umpire did not agree. He called a strike. Ken felt a jab of quick annoyance, but smothered it at once.

A fast hook came blazing in, and Ken almost had it figured right as it flashed in toward his knees. He met it squarely but too late. He blasted it outside the first-base line for a foul. Strike two. Slim Tucker had him in a hole.

And then Ken had a hunch that bordered upon downright certainty. There was good reason to believe that Tucker would try him out with a couple of wide pitches in the hope that Ken would cut at one of them, but, somehow or other, Ken had the feeling this would not happen. He believed he knew what was coming next.

At any rate, he gambled on it. He watched the windup like a hawk. He saw the tremendous energy Tucker appeared to pour into the throw, but this time Ken was not deceived by it.

When the flutterball came slowly toward the

plate, Ken was ready for it. His cleats were firmly planted in the earth. His balance was perfect, his muscles loose and limber.

He took a full, clean swing at Tucker's change of pace, and the following sharp crack produced a note of music no symphony could equal. The ball, a thin white streak, set out for center field. The fielder took one startled look, then whirled and sprinted wildly for the fence. He never had a chance. The ball crashed hard against the wall. Ken ended up on second base, and the baseball game was over.

The fans, of course, went wild, forgetting everything they had ever said or thought about Ken Holt. He was a great baseball player now, a hero.

The change in the Brickyard Gang was also amazing and complete. The Terriers swarmed out of the dugout and mobbed Ken. Needless to say, Borg did not join them, an omission Ken was glad to overlook. He was happy, and could get along without the sour note of Borg's presence.

9

Ken's luck stayed with him. During the remainder of the Ranger series he gave the Terrier fans a lot to yell about, and the yelling was all favorable. It boosted his morale and confidence, and that helped both his batting and his fielding. There was murder in his bat and magic in his glove. He was an overnight sensation.

It was the sort of thing that easily could swell a rookie's head. Ken felt the symptoms and fought against them, knowing himself to be as susceptible to extravagant praise as any normal man. Whenever he felt the tendency to strut, he always tried to catch himself in time, feeling the speculative eyes of the Terriers upon him. They were waiting for him to outgrow his hat.

That he didn't do so was probably the result of several factors. His common sense had something to do with it. So did Beezer Crane. The two of them had found a small apartment near the ballpark, and Beezer did his best to keep Ken realistic. Ken returned the favor when Beezer, in his first major-league start, defeated the Rangers in the final game. He permitted them only seven hits, to win 5–3. It was a nice performance, and Beezer knew it.

"Duck soup," he told Ken that evening in their apartment. "Nothing to it. What's all this talk about big-league batters being tough?"

Ken sighed and said, "So I've got competition, huh? Do you suppose this little joint'll hold a *pair* of big shots?" He took one of Beezer's gaudy neckties from the dresser, tossed it to him, and advised, "Here, pin this on yourself and pretend it's an orchid."

Beezer caught the tie and said, "Okay, okay, so I'm cocky."

"You are?" asked Ken with shocked amazement.

"A little," Beezer qualified.

"The Rangers were off stride today. Anybody could've tossed a beanbag past 'em."

"Hum-m-m," mused Beezer. Then he added plaintively, "Will it be all right if I just sleep here tonight? I'll be ever so quiet. I'll let you shave first in the morning. You'll never know I'm here. Really, Mr. Holt."

"That's better," approved Ken. "Just don't forget who's the big noise in this dugout."

"I won't . . . sir. I'll always remember that I'm rooming with the great Ken Holt, the wonder boy, who'll fall flat on his face when his luck runs out."

"Too true to be funny," Ken said with a rueful grin.

It was a pertinent thought, however, and Ken decided to push his luck while it was still running high. He called at Jake Tobin's office the following morning. Tobin was busy with paperwork, but he shoved it willingly aside when Ken came in.

"Sit down, Ken. What's on your mind? You look worried."

"Well," admitted Ken, "I am, a little. I've got a pretty big favor to ask of you."

"That's one of the things a baseball manager is

for," said Tobin philosophically. "What's on your mind?"

Ken rubbed his chin, not knowing quite where to start. Finally, jumping in with both feet, he said, "I want to find some tough kids and try to organize 'em into baseball teams."

"Huh?" said Tobin, startled.

"Well," said Ken, turning a little red, "I've had the idea in my mind for a long time. A lot of youngsters in tough districts get off on the wrong foot and turn into criminals because they haven't enough outside interests. Maybe I'm a little cracked on the subject, but it seems to me that if a lot of them were organized into an active baseball league, it would be bound to keep 'em out of a lot of trouble. Besides, I like to work with kids."

Tobin relighted his cigar while Ken watched him intently, wondering how the manager would react to such an unusual request from one of his own players. Tobin finally blew a smoke spiral toward the ceiling, eyed Ken steadily for a moment, then asked, "How would you go about it, Ken?"

Ken let his breath out slowly, finding encouragement in Tobin's tone. "I'd spend my mornings at it. I wouldn't let it interfere with my own baseball."

Tobin gave the matter careful thought. "If I could be sure of that part, I couldn't very well refuse."

"It might be worth a try," suggested Ken.

"It might," the manager agreed. "Go ahead, Ken. But if it affects your game, I'll have to call you off."

"Thanks," Ken told him. "Thanks a lot."

He had started to leave the office when Tobin called him back, and asked, "How do you plan to find these kids?"

"I'd intended to talk it over with the Commissioner of Recreation."

"Good idea! I happen to know him. Name's Greyson. Want me to phone him?"

"You bet I do."

An hour later Ken was in Henry Greyson's office. Greyson listened with interest to what Ken had to say, then admitted readily, "There are several districts, Mr. Holt, that ought to suit your purpose." He brought out a city map, spread it on the desk, and drew circles that enclosed several separated areas. He tapped one of the circles with his pencil and went on. "We feel this district is in real need of something of the sort you suggest. It had been included in our plans of expansion, but . . . Well," he shrugged apologetically, "we simply haven't reached it yet."

"May I have a go at it?" asked Ken.

"We'd be glad to have you. I'm sorry to say we can't be of any financial assistance to you at the moment, but I'm sure it could be arranged, once we are convinced you're on the right track and are making progress."

"I'd rather tackle it alone at first," said Ken. "It's something I've wanted to do for a long time, and I'd get a bigger kick out of it if I could do it without help. May I have this map?"

"Certainly, Mr. Holt. And the best of luck. I wish there were more men like you."

Ken gave Beezer a brief outline of his plans, knowing they would soon be public knowledge, if they were successful. Also, expecting that most of his mornings would ultimately be devoted to his plans, he saw no reason why his absence should confront Beezer with an unnecessary mystery. Beezer liked the idea.

"Want help?" he offered.

Ken turned him down, explaining that he wanted to try it alone at first.

He decided to start his experiment on Saturday

morning when the youngsters would be out of school. He was excited at the prospect, but told himself not to expect too much in the beginning. He located his objective on the map and started out.

Before leaving, he slipped a baseball in his pocket, a good ball, still white and almost new. It had been fouled into the screen and was slightly nicked, which made it unsuitable for use in a scheduled game. That tiny nick might grip the air just hard enough to impart a little extra curve to a pitch. The ball had therefore been discarded, to be used for practice only. The Terriers had more of these damaged balls than they could use. Ken had asked Tobin for this one some days ago, and the manager had said, "Help yourself."

Just why Ken took the ball along with him that day he didn't know. His plans were vague, to be formed by whatever circumstances he might encounter, if he encountered any worthy of a plan.

He got off the subway, walked awhile, and found himself in the sort of district he was seeking—dingy, overcrowded tenements, littered streets, a profusion of dirty children, and the constant jarring din of people who are forced to live without sufficient elbow room.

The sights and odors were familiar to Ken Holt because he had lived in such surroundings. He knew how these folks felt. He knew the underlying vein of dangerous discontent and fierce resentment against poverty, and knew it as the breeding ground for modes of thinking that could lead to crime.

He strolled along the sidewalk, avoiding push-carts piled with shabby merchandise, whose owners trundled them through the crowded street and cocked a watchful eye for customers. Small, playing children bumped against Ken's legs. He grinned and made the bumps as easy for them as he could.

He got the opportunity he had hoped for much sooner than he had anticipated. He had been prepared to spend days hunting a proper opening for his campaign, but he stumbled upon something now that looked as if it might have possibilities.

He came to an open space where a building had been torn down and not replaced. The ground had been leveled. It was reasonably smooth and was now serving as a baseball field despite its sadly limited proportions. Both first and third bases were directly against the blank brick walls of the buildings on each side, thereby eliminating most of left field and right field. This presented interesting fielding problems when the hits bounced off the walls like pool balls off a cushion. A moderate hit to center field would end up in the coal bunker of a fuel supply yard, and the grimy appearance of the outfielders suggested that they had retrieved numerous balls from the unhandy spot. The catcher's backstop was nothing but a tall packing case of thin wood with a few smaller boxes piled on top. It was directly against the sidewalk, because the pitcher threw in that direction.

Ken stopped to watch, joining the few loafers who had formed a gallery because they had nothing else to do. Ken's interest quickened as he sized up the ages of the players, most of them, he estimated, between eleven and fourteen. They were as tough a bunch of little rowdies as he could have hoped to find, but they were playing baseball with a noisy, avid zeal, and that was what Ken was looking for.

Ken knew from sound experience that youngsters like this would welcome no intrusion from an elder, certainly not from a stranger. They were using a ball covered with black tape. Ken fingered the smooth ball in his pocket, knowing he could not just walk up and hand it to them. They would probably grab the ball and run, figuring that Ken was crazy or might change his mind.

It began to appear, however, that this was the only chance he had. Maybe he would have the opportunity when the game broke up.

The catcher crouched behind the plate. His mask was a wire kitchen strainer padded with rags around the edges. His chest protector was a fitted piece of heavy roofing paper. His mitt was losing padding at the edges, but his attitude was businesslike as he squatted behind the plate using all the professional gestures he could remember.

He flashed the sign. The pitcher, a lanky boy in a red and green T-shirt, considered the signal carefully, then shook his head, inviting the catcher to try again.

The catcher, however, had no such intentions. His professional manner deserted him abruptly as he stood erect and yelled, "You throw the one I told you to, you meathead! If you don't I'll come out and bat ya in the teeth!"

This seemed to settle it. It appeared to be a matter of local etiquette all could understand. It also suggested that the catcher bossed the team, and that his fists were potent.

The pitcher said, "Sure, Butch," without resentment.

Butch squatted again, repeated the sign, and this time the pitcher nodded. He wound up like a contortionist, managed to get untangled, and the ball came toward the plate.

It was a trifle high, but the batter took a cut at it. He swung mightily and sent a long high foul behind him. The backstop was unequal to the job expected of it. The ball sailed over it with room to spare. It kept on sailing, crossed the street, and hurtled toward a grocery store upon the other side.

Ken held his breath in worried apprehension that was justified at once. The ball crashed through a window, luckily a small one. The damage actually was slight, but the immediate effects were no less than terrific.

Ken turned back to the baseball field, wondering what the boys would do. He should have known, because he had done the same himself not many years ago. They scattered and ran with the smooth coordination born of constant practice. They left the place like flies shooed off a lump of sugar. Although Ken turned quickly, he was barely in time to see the last of them scoot off into the safety of the coal yard.

His attention snapped back to the grocery store, drawn there by sounds emerging from within. They were strong sounds, wrathful sounds, loud bellowings from powerful lungs, which swelled in volume as their owner neared the entrance.

Ken glued his eyes with active interest on the doorway, expecting no less than a gorilla to rush out, maybe two of them. He was therefore taken by surprise when a small round man popped out as if someone had fired him from a slingshot.

In shape the man was something like an egg, a likeness increased by the long white grocer's apron that almost touched the ground. It concealed his legs, making it appear as if he had gained his speed by means of wheels.

His face was round and swarthy, brick red, now, with fury. A magnificent black mustache floated in the breeze he had created. The ends of the mustache jiggled violently with each new roar. He seemed too small to hold such rage, too small to move so fast. He must have had a running start, Ken reasoned logically, a good build-up sprint from the rear of the store to have attained such great momentum, a momentum he could not control.

This was demonstrated when he reached the sidewalk. A pushcart piled with tinware ambled unsuspectingly into his path. The grocer tried to miss it, but he couldn't change his course entirely. The best he could manage was a sideswipe which barely slowed him down but which upset the cart and sent the tinware crashing to the street to add its contribution to the uproar. Thereupon the owner of the pushcart raised his voice in towering fury. He too had power and volume almost equal to the grocer's.

The grocer, meanwhile, reached the empty baseball field and, finding it deserted, checked his speed. He plowed to a frustrated stop, did a few hopping dance steps, and shook his fists at the innocent coal pile. He roared a few final threats, then subsided into spluttering Italian.

The pushcart owner had reached the scene by this time. He was about to hit the grocer on the head with a tin coffeepot, when Ken, seeing no one else intended to, moved in to interfere. He held the pair apart and took a blow on the shoulder from the coffeepot. Before the pot swinger had time to wind up for another, Ken said, "I'll pay for all the damage."

Ken was spared long negotiations by the arrival of the policeman on the beat, a burly man with a strong jaw and patient eyes. He removed his cap, mopped his perspiring forehead, and inquired, "*Now* what?"

The grocer and the pushcart man burst into speech.

The policeman turned to Ken and said, "*You* tell it."

Ken told him briefly what had happened, ending with his offer to pay the damages. The policeman looked relieved.

"Those kids," he said with a long-suffering air. Then he turned to the grocer. "How much, Luigi?"

Luigi struggled with himself and said, "Three buck."

"How about you, Herman?" asked the cop.

Herman seemed to think three dollars would also take care of his mental anguish and the few dents in his tinware. Ken gave them each five dollars and won a pair of lasting friends. The policeman shooed them back to their respective trades, dispersed the small crowd, but seemed in no hurry to return to his own job.

"Those kids," he repeated wearily. "They drive me nuts, but I guess it ain't their fault, poor little punks. There's no place for 'em to play down here except on the streets. I guess I should've made 'em quit playin' baseball on that little lot, but I didn't have the heart."

"Aren't there any bigger lots around here for 'em to play in?" asked Ken.

"Yeah. Just behind those coal piles is a lot of space, but the guy that runs the coal yard won't let 'em use it. He hates kids."

"Does he own the yard?"

"No, just manages it."

"Who owns it?"

"Big shot by the name of Holden. He owns several factories. That's where he uses this coal."

"Somebody ought to talk to him."

"Who'd do it?"

"I will."

"*You?*" said the cop, astounded. "What for?"

Ken liked the policeman's looks, so he told him what he had in mind. The man beamed his approval.

"What's your name?" he asked. "Mine's Jim Burk."

"Mine's Holt. Ken Holt."

Burk stared at him. "You wouldn't be the Terriers' center fielder, would you?"

"I guess I would," admitted Ken.

Burk was satisfactorily impressed. They talked baseball for a while, and when Burk finally felt the call of duty, he told Ken before leaving, "I'm with you all the way on this kid business. Just call on me if I can help."

"I will."

10

After Burk had strolled off along his beat, Ken removed one of the small boxes from the backstop, placed it at first base, sat down on it, and leaned against the wall to wait. He was waiting for the youngsters, certain in his own mind that they would come back.

He knew they were not far away. He could almost feel the pressure of their eyes as they stared at him from hiding places, held by curiosity, which was what he counted on, the avid curiosity of young animals.

He knew their curiosity would expand, and could almost picture what was taking place. They were wondering who he was, what he was doing there, and why he had helped them. Soon they would be daring one another to come out and solve the mystery. He also had a good idea who would be the first to take the dare.

He was right. The catcher, Butch, soon made an appearance. He came from the direction of the coal pile, walking with an exaggerated swagger he hoped would hide the nervousness he dared not show before his pals. They were undoubtedly watching every movement. Ken eyed his approach with studied unconcern. Butch finally reached the spot, and planted himself truculently in front of Ken.

"Who told you you could sit on that there box?" demanded Butch.

Ken kept his eyes expressionless as they rested upon Butch. He saw a stocky youngster in his early teens, a boy who wanted to be tough. He had sandy hair, wide, rebellious blue eyes. The whole expression of the face was hostile, but underneath that there was something Ken Holt liked. The eyes were steady, clear, and honest, at that moment. They could easily remain so, but Ken had seen such eyes in other youngsters turn dangerous and hard when bad environment and worse companions had their effect on them.

Impatient at Ken's silence, Butch demanded, "What's the matter, mister? Can't you talk?"

"Yeah," said Ken mildly. "And I heard you the first time. I get you young punks out of a jam and save you from a rap, and you won't even let me use your box to sit on. What sort of a guy are you?"

A flicker of embarrassment showed in Butch's eyes as he absorbed Ken's logic. Some of the others, emboldened by the example Butch had set, began to move into the picture. Butch, encouraged by their presence and by Ken's apparent mildness, took a grip on his slipping confidence.

"Nobody asked you to stick your nose in," he told Ken. "We can get out of our own jams." Then, curiosity getting the better of him, he added, "Why'd you do it?"

Ken shrugged. "I guess because I was a sucker. I must have figured I was playing with square guys. Looks like I was wrong."

"We *are* square guys!" Butch said hotly. "But you still stuck your nose into our business. What's your racket?"

Ken hid a grin. "No racket, kid. I just happen to like baseball. In fact, I play it for a living."

"I'll bet you do," jeered Butch. "I guess you'll tell us next you're with the Terriers."

"You guessed it, kid," said Ken.

Butch was obviously shaken, but, having taken a definite stand before his pals, he knew he had to hold his ground. He turned to his gallery with a broad wink that was supposed to mean, Now watch me show this phony up. Facing Ken again, he said, "Now what d'ya know. The guy says he's a Terrier. Now don't tell me, mister. Lemme guess. Maybe you're Ken Holt, the new rookie fireball."

"Sure," said Ken. "That's me."

Butch exploded with derisive mirth that turned out to be short-lived. One of his friends was staring hard at Ken. The boy said in a tight, awe-filled voice, "Butch, it—it *is* Ken Holt."

Butch whirled on him and yelled, "You're nuts!" Then he turned to the others. "Did ya hear 'im? Did ya hear what Mikey said? He's nuts, ain't he?"

But Mikey doggedly held his ground. "I ain't nuts. You know I found a buck the other day, and you know I spent it on a bleacher seat for the Ranger game. I was sittin' right behind him in center field.

It's him, all right. It's Ken Holt!" His voice by this time was squeaky with excitement.

Butch's eyes took on the look of a person who knows he is losing an unequal struggle. They also reflected the awed expression in the eyes of the others.

"You—you are Ken Holt?" he demanded thickly.

"Sure, Butch. I'm Holt."

Butch battled with the incredible information while suspicion crept gradually back into his eyes. He finally said, "If you are Ken Holt, what're you doing here?"

It was logic worthy of an older person. Ken considered the question carefully. He knew it would never do to tell the truth—that he was sorry for them, that they were heading for the rocks, that he wanted to help them.

"Maybe I'll want to be a big-league manager some day," he said, "and I've got to start somewhere. I can't start at the top, so I guess I'd better start from the bottom, with a team of kids, for instance. I saw you kids playing, and figured maybe I could move in now and then and teach you a few things I've learned from Jake Tobin. I'd get good experience that way."

Ken hoped he had hit the right note, and he had. The youngsters seemed to find the explanation thoroughly plausible. Butch nodded sagely. "Good idea," he said.

"Maybe I can find you a bigger lot to play on, and wrangle you some equipment, gloves and things."

Ken saw he had gone a step too far. Suspicion came again into Butch's eyes, proving he was too shrewd to believe in miracles. Catching the expression, Ken took the baseball from his pocket. "Here," he said. "Take this for a starter."

Butch's eyes bugged out. He reached for the baseball gingerly, as if for something valuable and fragile. He turned it over in his hand and breathed, "My gosh!"

The others crowded around him. He released the ball reluctantly, and it passed from hand to hand. Ken let his breath out with relief. He was making headway. He believed he had a solid toehold now, but his satisfaction ended suddenly.

One of the youngsters yelped, "Butch! Here comes your brother!" Then to Ken, as if announcing the arrival of the President of the United States, he said, "Nick Browski."

Ken suspected trouble, and nothing about Nick Browski changed his mind as he watched the approach of Butch's brother. There was no mistaking the relationship. He was a large facsimile of Butch, but hardened to authentic toughness by his added years. Ken judged him at nineteen or twenty a tempered product of the district.

Ken's mind worked fast as Nick came closer. There were several things he was sure of. By glancing at the faces of the boys, the looks of pride and adulation there, Ken knew Nick Browski was their hero, a greater hero to them than the baseball player, Holt. Nick's very presence shoved Ken to the background.

Ken also guessed that Nick was dangerously jealous of his prestige with the youngsters. It showed in his expression, in the truculence of his outthrust jaw. He came upon the scene with the air of a man who was looking for a chance to settle matters with anyone who tried to interfere in his own private territory. He planted himself, stocky and barrel-chested, in front of Ken. Ken sat relaxed upon the box, and kept his face expressionless.

"What's your business, Mac?" demanded Nick.

"Ask the kids."

"I'm askin' *you.*"

Butch gathered courage to inform his brother, "It's Ken Holt, Nick. Ken Holt of the Terriers."

Nick flicked a glance at Butch, then brought his eyes back searchingly to Ken. He studied him intently, nodded and said, "Yeah, it's Holt. His picture was in all the papers."

The proof of identity didn't help Ken's cause. It made it worse, and Ken knew why. It made him a person to be reckoned with, a man who might replace Nick as a hero with the boys. Nick's face went even harder. He turned and snarled, "You dumb little punks! Why would a guy like Holt waste time with you? There's somethin' fishy about this. He's got a racket, and if you kids had any brains you'd know it."

He watched the words sink in, then whirled on Ken again. "Get out!" he ordered. "Get out before I knock you silly!"

It was a hard moment for Ken Holt, hard for him to think of anything but the terrific urge to teach Nick Browski a few manners. He came within an ace of following the urge, but a sixth sense held him off. If he fought and defeated Nick, right here before these youngsters, Ken knew they would hate him from the bottom of their hearts. He would lose the ground he had gained and never get it back again.

Ken also had a strange reluctance, angry as he was at Nick, to bring his small world toppling about his ears. The worship of these boys meant a lot to Nick. And who was Ken to spoil it?

It was a hard decision, but Ken made it with a shrug. He got up off the box, maintaining a nice balance just in case Nick should decide to throw a punch. But Nick seemed satisfied with matters as they stood. He jerked his thumb in a gesture of dismissal. "Beat it, Mac!"

Nick's tone and gesture almost snapped Ken's self-control. The urge to have it out with Nick came back full force. Why not? As matters stood, he would never be able to face these boys again, even though there was no sign of contempt in their expressions at the moment. They took it as a matter of course that Nick Browski could order anyone around.

Nevertheless, Ken knew his plans were ruined. Or were they? Wasn't there a loophole?

He said to Nick, "Let's go somewhere we can talk."

The youngsters failed to catch the actual meaning of the words. Nick, wiser in such matters, caught it promptly. His eyes showed quick surprise, then satisfaction.

"Sure, Mac, sure," he said. "I know a place."

He led the way. Ken followed at his shoulder.

"You're askin' for it, Mac. We don't like strangers snoopin' in this neighborhood, and when I get through with you you'll wish you'd ducked out when you had the chance." Then he added curiously, "Why didn't you?"

"I don't like guys who try to throw their weight around. When they try it on me, I've got to find out what they've got to back it up."

"I've got plenty, Mac. You'll need new teeth when I get through with you."

"If I figured it that way, Nick, I wouldn't be here. Would I?"

"No," Nick conceded. "Maybe not. Maybe you're just dumb."

Nick left the crowded street and led the way through a narrow, rubbish-littered alley that brought them to the railroad tracks behind the coal dump. He selected an empty coal gondola, looked carefully around to assure himself they were not observed, then snapped to Ken, "Inside, sucker. Make it snappy!"

Ken hurried up the iron rungs on the gondola's side and dropped inside the roomy car. Nick followed on his heels. There was lots of space inside, a perfect spot for a private brawl.

Nick Browski wasted no more time. He squared away, said, "This is it, Mac!" and came in swinging.

It was the type of attack Ken had hoped for. It confirmed his early hunch that Nick was nothing but a slugger. Most men of that build, powerful shoulders and short arms, could be counted on to fight that way, resorting to their bull-like strength and the battering force of their big fists.

Nick failed to catch Ken Holt off balance. Ken had his feet braced solidly to meet the rush, and he surprised Nick even further by failing to give ground.

Ken let his knees bend sharply, kept his body forward and his fists down low. Nick's sizzling swings passed harmlessly over his head. Nick's body collided heavily with Ken's shoulder, and while Nick hung there for an instant, Ken's two fists came blasting up into his belly.

Nick grunted from the shock but weathered it.

His midriff was well ridged with muscle, but the blows had hurt him just the same. He moved back, sucking hard for wind, glaring at Ken with fury and surprise. Nick kept his guard up, expecting Ken to follow his advantage, but Ken watched him, poker-faced, and let him catch his breath.

Nick was baffled. This was not the ruthless style of fighting he was used to. A flicker of doubt showed in his eyes but was quickly gone. He charged again, this time flailing uppercuts in the hope that Ken would crouch again.

Ken didn't. His reach was inches longer than Nick Browski's, and he took full advantage of it. He extended a long left arm, fingers open. He let Nick's nose batter hard against the heel of his palm. It was a painful blow but not too damaging.

Tears spurted to Nick's eyes and he went wild with rage. The air was full of Browski fists, and Ken had trouble for a moment keeping out of danger. He took a couple of hard blows on the shoulder, a glancing set of knuckles off his skull, but managed by swift footwork and a jabbing left to neutralize Nick's savage swings.

No man could hold the pace Nick had set himself. His breath was whistling from his lungs, his punches were losing force. His eyes turned glassy with fatigue and with the growing knowledge that things were not turning out as he had expected. He knew, by this time, that Ken was the better fighter. But Nick was game. He kept on trying, and Ken knew the only way to stop the brawl was by a knockout.

He coolly watched for his chance, and when the moment came he flashed a wicked right across Nick's shoulder. It crashed against his jaw to spin him half around, out cold upon his feet.

Ken moved in fast to save Nick from a header to the steel floor of the car. He caught him as he toppled, eased him down, and braced his back against the side.

Ken waited anxiously for Nick to come around. A lot depended upon how Nick Browski would react to what had happened to him. He was tough, all through. But had the toughness killed the spark of honesty that Ken had noticed in the younger brother, a spark Nick had probably owned himself as Butch's age?

Ken knew from his own experience that Nick Browski's gang was governed by a certain code of ethics. But, and the question was a big one, would Nick apply those ethics to his present problem?

It was a question, however, that would soon be answered. Nick showed signs of returning consciousness. His legs began to twitch, and shortly after that his eyes came slowly open. He shook his head and pawed a hand across his face. It left a streak of coal dust. His thoughts began to focus. The dazed look left his eyes and they came to rest upon Ken Holt.

There was no encouragement to Ken in Nick's expression. Nick's eyes turned hot and ugly as memory flooded back. He made an effort to get up, but his muscles failed him. He leaned back, glared at Ken, and said, "You won't get away with it."

Ken squatted on his heels against the opposite car wall. He took his time before replying. Finally he said, "We had a fight, a private fight. It's nobody's business but yours and mine. I'll keep my trap shut, Nick, because I'm not a heel."

Nick grappled with that statement, and Ken, watching him carefully, decided he had made the right approach. Nick certainly did not like the idea of being defeated, but, as matters stood, Ken believed he could accept the situation and could even feel a certain grim respect for the man who had knocked him out. There was no particular disgrace connected with it so long as no one knew about it but Ken Holt and Nick.

However, if the news got out, if Nick's friends and the youngsters should learn about it, Nick would have a serious problem on his hands, a blot on his cherished reputation. Maybe he could live it down and maybe he couldn't. It was of vital importance to Nick Browski that the news should not leak out, and it all depended on Ken Holt.

Sensing this, Ken forced the issue, taking advantage of Nick's temporary indecision. He repeated quietly, "I'm not a heel." Then he threw the question directly in the other's teeth. "Am I, Nick?"

The offensive strategy took Nick by surprise, forcing his eyes to meet Ken's squarely in a searching stare. It also forced an honest grudging answer, as if the words were dragged from him against his will. He growled, "Okay, you're not a squealer."

"And here's another angle," Ken went on, pushing his advantage. "I almost tangled with you back there in front of the kids."

Nick's eyebrows drew together in a puzzled frown. He finally said suspiciously, "I'll bite. Why didn't you?"

"I figured I might have the edge on you, a longer

reach, and I know how to box. If I'd tangled with you then and had proved my point, I'd have been a first-class rat, because those kids think you're tops. I don't like to be pushed around, so I waited till we could settle things in private."

A look of incredulity passed across Nick's face. He checked it promptly with a sneer, and said, "Am I supposed to believe that tripe?"

"Suit yourself."

"Nuts," said Nick.

He got to his feet and started toward the ladder at the end of the car. Ken let him go, fearing for an instant that he had figured Nick all wrong. He saw Nick hesitate, then stop. Ken let his breath out softly in relief. Nick turned and asked, scowling, "What's your racket, Holt? What were you doing with those kids?"

Ken had Nick's interest now. Beneath his truculence Ken sensed his slow conviction that Ken Holt was on the level. Ken knew now that he had played his cards right, after all. He played the rest of them with care.

He told Nick what he had in mind, the organization of a baseball league among the youngsters, and how he hoped to find a better diamond for them and some new equipment. His own deep interest in the matter found its way into his voice, and the fire of his enthusiasm touched Nick briefly. His eyes showed a flicker of sharp interest, but he smothered the expression quickly, keeping his face hard.

Ken also read resentment in Nick's eyes, the look of a man who sees the threat of losing something he values.

Ken spoke quickly. "I'd need a lot of help, someone to really run things for me, someone to keep the kids in line. That job's too big for me. They need a boss, a manager. Do you know where I could find one, Nick?"

Nick's face took on a fresh protective mask of hardness. He spat indifferently upon the coal dust in the car. He shrugged and said, "That's your headache, Mac."

He turned abruptly, climbed out of the car, and disappeared. Ken left a short time later, smiling grimly to himself. He believed he had made a little progress, but he knew the road ahead was still a rocky one.

11

Ken's next move toward the fulfillment of his plans was a visit to the office of John Holden, the man who owned the coal yard.

Ken started upon the mission with a reasonable amount of confidence, which soon began to disappear. His first misgivings stemmed from the discovery that Mr. Holden was a very wealthy man, if such a fact could be assumed from the extent and luxury of his offices, which occupied a full floor of a Broad Street building.

His self-assurance received another blow when he saw the receptionist in the outer lobby. She was young, beautiful, and highly polished. Ken's experience with girls had been negligible.

She eyed him with professional disinterest as he approached the desk. It was obviously her job to discourage unknown vistors. She raised blank eyes to Ken.

Ken swallowed and said hesitantly, "I—I'd like to see Mr. Holden."

Her expression indicated that lots of people would like to see Mr. Holden. "Do you have an appointment?"

"No."

Her eyelids merely flickered, but Ken understood. No one, of course, but a pitiful, half-witted clown could expect to see Mr. John Holden without an appointment. She sighed and asked, "Your name?"

"Ken Holt."

"Your business?"

Ken said, "I'm a baseball player."

She looked startled, then said coldly, "I was referring to your business with Mr. Holden."

"Baseball," said Ken doggedly.

She looked a little harried, uncertain, too. This was something new in her experience, something she had never had to cope with.

Ken caught all this and, aided by a slowly rising

anger, pushed his luck. "Tell Mr. Holden I want to talk to him about baseball."

"Well, I . . . I don't know. I . . ."

"Tell him!" Ken snapped sharply.

She glared at him but reached for the phone. When John Holden was on the other end she said a trifle shakily, "There's a . . . a man out here by the name of Ken Holt. He says he's a baseball player, and he wants to talk to you about baseball."

Ken heard a lusty voice come through the earpiece. "Holt!" it roared. "Ken Holt? The Terrier? Send 'im in! Send 'im in! What're you waiting for?"

"Ye . . . yes, sir." She replaced the phone, stared at Ken, and said dazedly, "Through that door, sir. First office on the right."

Ken followed her directions, knowing that this was sheer good luck. John Holden was obviously a baseball fan, a rabid one. He had heard of the Terriers' rookie outfielder, and obviously wanted to meet him face to face.

Ken's reasoning was sound. John Holden, a robust man in his early sixties, pumped Ken's hand with enthusiasm, led him to a chair, and started to talk baseball. Presently he asked, "What do you want to see me about?"

Ken told him briefly. The older man listened carefully, nodding from time to time. When Ken had finished, Holden said, "A cinch. I'll have 'em start cleaning up the yard tomorrow. There'll be room for a full-sized diamond with plenty of outfield for kid sluggers. I'll build a backstop, put in a home plate, pitching slab, and bases. I'll try to have it ready by Saturday morning so you can present it to the kids yourself. We'll keep it a secret from them until then."

Ken, confused by his success, could only stammer, "It . . . it's more than I'd hoped for. I . . . Well, thanks a lot."

"Forget it. How about balls, gloves, bats, and uniforms?"

"I'd hoped to attend to that myself, not all at once . . . but as fast as I could afford it."

"Forget that, too. If you can get things organized, I'll supply the equipment. I can afford it and it'll be a pleasure. I'd like to do my part to give the kids a break."

Ken left John Holden's office feeling as if he were walking upon fleecy clouds. Things were breaking so spectacularly in his favor that he began to fear there was a catch to it. It didn't make sense, somehow, that the unhappiness of his past years could be replaced by his satisfaction of the moment.

It was a sobering consideration which gave him food for thought, and checked his elation. He warned himself that he was still treading upon shaky ground. He must keep his hopes in reasonable restraint, take nothing for granted, and face each problem as it came.

He spent a restless week in anticipation of the following Saturday, but the restlessness added zest to his baseball. He maintained the pace he had set in the early games, and held his place in the fickle affections of the fans.

So far, so good. Nevertheless, apprehension was gnawing at the edges of his nerves on Saturday morning when he approached the vicinity of John Holden's coal yards. There was no way of knowing how he would be received; that would depend largely on the attitude Nick Browski chose to assume.

When Ken reached his destination, he got a quick lift of satisfaction at the promptness with which John Holden had fulfilled his promise. The big lot had been cleared and smoothed. A baseball diamond had been laid out, with an adequate backstop behind the plate.

The diamond, however, was unoccupied. Butch Browski and his friends were gathered on the sideline, staring at the field with envious, longing eyes, wondering who would have the use of it. Ken also noted, with a tightening of his muscles, that Nick Browski was there. It was just as well, decided Ken. Might as well get things settled now as any time. He walked up and said, "Hi, fellows."

Eyes swung in his direction. There was an abrupt charged silence. Then the eyes of the youngsters turned toward Nick. They had heard Nick order Ken away the previous week, and so far as they knew the situation was unchanged. They were looking for swift fireworks.

Nick scowled at Ken, spat upon the ground, then turned back to the boys. "Relax," he told them gruffly. "The guy's okay."

The youngsters stared incredulously. Nick snarled at them, "I told ya, didn't I? The guy's okay."

They received the verdict with some disappointment. They had been hoping for a fight. Then, with that prospect ruled out, they began to regard Ken with a rising interest, a new respect. Obviously he had passed the acid test.

Ken let his breath out slowly, trying to keep relief

from showing on his face. He said, "This diamond's for you kids to use."

"Who ya kiddin'?" Nick demanded.

"No one. The place belongs to a big shot by the name of Holden. I talked to him last Monday. He's a baseball fan, and a pushover for a deal like this. He likes kids, so he fixed this place for you."

Expressions ranged from incredulity to black suspicion. The eyes of the youngsters were on Nick again. Nick gave the matter careful thought before he spoke. "It's on the level. Go ahead."

The boys let out a yell and charged upon the diamond. Ken, watching their wild enthusiasm, felt the warmth of satisfaction travel through his veins. He glanced at Nick, whose eyes were also on the diamond, and noted without surprise that the protective mask of hardness was no longer on his face. He also seemed to be deriving pleasure from the moment.

Ken said, "It's a good start, Nick."

Nick turned. He made an effort to replace the mask, but he failed. Instead, he nodded and said, "Yeah."

"We've still got a lot of work ahead of us."

"A lot of work," conceded Nick. Then, after a

brief battle with himself, he said, "You can count me in."

"A deal," said Ken, and let it go at that.

There was, as Ken had said, a lot of work ahead, and he found Nick's help invaluable. Nick was able to suggest many shortcuts as his interest in the work developed to a point that almost equaled Ken's. There was a quality of straight thinking in Nick Browski, an inherent fairness, and a streak of sentiment beneath his toughness.

One day he said, "I guess I'm just a cream puff after all, Ken. I want to see my brother, Butch, get headed in the right direction. He's a tough little monkey, but this baseball stuff is keeping him out of the gutters and giving him something good to think about." He rubbed his chin, then admitted sheepishly, "Maybe it's about time I set him a good example."

"It won't be easy," said Ken, speaking from experience.

"You're telling me! There'll be trouble when I start breakin' away from the crowd I been runnin' with. They won't like it."

"No," said Ken. "They probably won't."

This guess was soon confirmed by the bruised

features and skinned knuckles Nick displayed from time to time.

"Looks like you've been arguing with your pals," Ken said.

"Yeah, I have," admitted Nick. "But it don't make much sense. I have to bat 'em down, but not for the reason I figured on."

"I don't quite get it," Ken admitted.

"I told you it was screwy. They're tryin' to muscle in. They figure I'm havin' some fun they're missin'. They figure that managing the Busters makes sort of a big shot out of me, and some of 'em want to be big shots too."

Ken considered this with a slow grin of satisfaction. He finally said, "I like the sound of that."

Nick showed signs of annoyance, so Ken hastened to explain. "I'm planning on at least a six-team league down here, and all the teams will need good managers."

"Okay," growled Nick. "But if you think I'm goin' to let any of these—"

"Keep your shirt on," Ken interrupted. "We've also got to have somebody who knows the ropes down here to act as general manager of all the teams, somebody to boss the works. I was figuring you for that job, if you thought you could swing it."

"What d'ya mean, if I can swing it?"

"I mean, do you want the job?"

"Sure I want it."

"You're in. Do you think you can find six good men for team managers?"

Greatly mollified, Nick considered the matter with the soberness of a newborn executive. He said at last, "Sure, I can find 'em. I can keep 'em in line, too, and make 'em work."

So the work of organizing the league got under way. They tackled the adjoining neighborhood first, sensibly worried because they knew what they were getting into.

The boys there, led by Monk Givanni, were natural enemies of the youngsters led by Butch. Miniature wars, vicious and often bloody, were not uncommon between the rival gangs, and Ken's optimistic hope was to bring the kids together on the baseball diamond, to let them settle their differences in an organized manner rather than with their fists.

It was a ticklish job beset with jealousy and hate. Nevertheless, aided by Nick's considerable reputation and by the willing influence of John Holden,

Ken was able to supply Monk Givanni's gang with a suitable layout, and to organize a team which called itself the Scorpions. Butch and his friends had decided to call their club the Busters. The next experiment was to match the Busters and the Scorpions in a game.

It was scheduled for a Saturday morning. Ken and Nick were both on edge when the time arrived, knowing they were faced with something only slightly less hazardous than herding a group of lions into a den of tigers.

Both teams were equipped with first-rate mitts, bats, and balls. Ken had hoped to surprise them with uniforms that day. He had been promised that the uniforms would be delivered at the field, but their arrival was delayed and he was forced to start the game without them, grateful that he had not raised the youngsters' hopes of making their debut in full regalia.

Tension was high as the game got under way. Nick Browski had accepted the precarious job of umpire. By dint of personality, a loud voice, and constant watchfulness he managed to keep the two teams in order for two and a half innings.

Monk Givanni was pitching for the Scorpions

and was turning in a good performance. The boy showed promise. He had speed and the makings of a curve but also a tendency to wildness.

The Scorpions had pushed across a run in the first and one in the second. They went scoreless in their top of the third, and the Busters came to bat in their half of the inning, seething at their inability to score and at the Scorpions' growing cockiness.

Stubby Klein, the Buster shortstop, led off with a single. The Busters began to yell for a run, but their second man popped out to third. He slunk back to the bench, scorned by his teammates and jeered by the Scorpions.

The third man grounded out to the first baseman, advancing Stubby to second, and the Busters' hopes now rested upon Butch. He strode to the plate, spat on his hands, then covered himself with glory by hitting a booming double to right field, scoring Stubby.

Monk Givanni turned to glare at Butch, taking the matter as a personal insult. Butch put a thumb in each ear, wiggled his fingers, and favored Monk with a loud raspberry. Monk started for him, but Nick grabbed Monk by the shoulder and pushed him back upon the mound. Nick turned to Butch and roared, "Shut up, or I'll come out there and boot you in the pants!"

Peace was temporarily restored, but Monk, feeling the effects of Butch's double, served a wide ball to the batter. Butch set sail for third, slid in under the throw, stood up and leered triumphantly at Monk. Monk paled slightly from his effort at restraint, but pulled himself together and threw a fast one.

It was fast enough, but wild as a wolverine. The catcher made a jump for it and missed. He followed the ball in scrambling panic to the backstop. Monk charged in to cover the plate, while Butch came sprinting in from third.

Monk spread himself out as wide as possible to block the rubber, howling, meanwhile, for the ball. The Scorpion catcher did his best but the throw was late. Monk did not even touch it. He had no chance as Butch came sliding in like a small tornado.

His body crashed against Monk's legs. Monk sailed in the air and came down on top of Butch. There was no way of knowing which one made the first aggressive move, because when the dust had cleared Butch and Monk were tangled in a snarling ball, fighting like a pair of alley cats.

The Scorpions with glad yells came surging from

the field. The Busters, with equally glad yells, came surging from the bench. They met in a happy welter of flying fists, baseball forgotten in the eager urge to battle.

It happened with such suddenness that Ken was taken by surprise. His emotions teetered between anger and a sick regret that baseball, in its first big chance, had failed to keep these youngsters from flying at each other's throats.

His first impulse was to haul the two teams apart, but he soon saw that it would be useless to try. Nick Browski was testing that technique, cuffing the opponents right and left, but he might as well have tried to subdue a hornets' nest.

And then a greater danger threatened. Both the Busters and the Scorpions had plenty of adult rooters. They were enjoying the equal fight right now, but if the tide should turn one way or another, the adults were easily capable of taking sides, a development that would mean a full-scale brawl.

Ken forced his numbed brain into action. He looked about him, weighing possibilities. Then he saw a small delivery truck pull up on the field, and he recognized the name upon the truck. The uniforms were here!

He hurried to the center of the melee, captured

Nick's attention, and said a few swift words to him. Nick bellowed, "Hold it, kids! The uniforms are here!"

Ken's impulse was sound. The announcement had a magic effect. A score of fists were stopped in mid-air. The wondrous word, "Uniforms!" passed from lip to lip and grew in volume. Eyes turned toward Nick. Nick pointed toward the truck, and the boys, the fight forgotten, stampeded in that direction.

Ken got there first. He helped the driver pile the bundles on the ground, while the youngsters stood around with avid eyes.

Butch yelped, "Let's see 'em, Mr. Holt!"

"Yeah. Let's see 'em," Monk said shrilly.

Ken said, "Okay," and selected a pair of uniforms. He displayed a deep-red suit with "*Busters*" spread across the chest in orange letters. The other was a green outfit with "*Scorpions*" in lemon-yellow blazoned on the shirt. The youngsters gazed with bulging eyes, their exclamations of amazement muted by their deep emotion.

"Can . . . can we have 'em now?" Butch asked in humble tones.

Ken faced the circle with blank eyes. "No. You don't deserve them. You may never get 'em."

He let the words take hold, watching the shock of them sink deep into the youngsters' minds. Judging his timing carefully, he said, "These suits are for baseball players, for guys who know what baseball means, who play the game according to the rules. They're not for you."

He glanced at Nick. Nick took his cue and said, "Ken's right. These suits are too good for punks. What'll we do with the suits, Ken?"

"Can you find a place to keep 'em?"

"Sure."

"Hide 'em away then. Maybe we'll find kids someday who deserve 'em."

"But . . . but, Mr. Holt," Butch blurted, "they're our suits. We deserve 'em."

"Ha!" said Ken.

Butch wilted.

Monk Givanni stepped into the breach. "We ain't punks, Mr. Holt. Won't you give us another chance to get the suits?"

"Yeah," said Butch, getting the idea fast, "can't we have another chance?"

Ken let his eyes move back and forth from Butch to Monk, wondering just how far he dared to go. Finally deciding to take the risk, he said, "Will you promise to play baseball all the way? No fights?"

They swallowed hard, but nodded.

"Will you shake hands to make it a tight bargain?"

That was the risky part. Ken saw the muscles of the two boys grow tense in protest, but Butch came through. He stuck his hand out. Monk, hesitating briefly, met it. It was a short, uncordial handshake, but Ken counted it a victory.

"Take a week to think it over," he advised. "We'll give it another try next Saturday."

Despite numerous apprehensions during the intervening days, Ken's judgment was vindicated when the game was finally played. There were hair-trigger moments, to be sure, but the youngsters satisfied their rivalry by playing baseball rather than by throwing punches. The Scorpions won 10–6 behind the superior pitching of Monk Givanni.

The Busters took their licking in bad grace, but they took it peaceably, which, so far as Ken was concerned, was the vitally important part. They had earned their uniforms, and Ken felt he had made a tremendous stride in the right direction.

It was the turning point that seemed to be the foundation for the progress that followed. News of the Busters and Scorpions spread and Ken and Nick were able to organize four more teams.

Nick, true to his prediction, found willing and able managers for the teams, and the managers accepted Ken's authority without question. Ken did his best to make them like him and succeeded.

He formed the six teams into the Morning League, which began to function smoothly under the direct supervision of Nick Browski. The league began its schedule at the end of the school term. The games were played in the morning, making it possible for Ken to attend them. He had to use considerable diplomacy in dividing his time among the teams in order to prevent jealousy, but he managed to spend some time at each game every morning he was in the city. When the Terriers were on the road, Nick handled the Morning League efficiently. It began to look as if Ken's dream were coming true.

Jake Tobin watched the experiment with a critical eye, primarily interested in the effect it might have on Ken himself. As long as Ken behaved himself and kept his batting average above .300, Tobin was content to let him pursue his hobby.

12

The wall of reserve still existed between Ken and the other Terriers, but they treated him with a qualified respect that established him as a valuable member of the club.

The exception was Cy Borg. The big right fielder made no open show of enmity, but his attitude of chill aloofness sometimes jangled on Ken's nerves.

More than once he caught Borg's gaze upon him. On these occasions there was curious speculation in Borg's eyes, but he always averted his stare before Ken could analyze the expression to his satisfaction.

Borg's attitude was disturbing, but Ken did little

worrying about it. And then something happened that made the threat of what Cy Borg might do seem meaningless and pallid by comparison.

It happened late one afternoon. The Terriers had just won a close 3–2 decision from the Boston Minutemen. Beezer Crane had turned in a fine five-hit performance on the mound, and Ken had drilled in the winning run in the bottom of the ninth. Leaving Beezer to the lengthy process of having his pitching arm massaged, Ken left the clubhouse feeling like a million dollars.

A crowd of dyed-in-the-wool fans were still lingering about the door waiting for a glimpse, an autograph, or perhaps a word of greeting from their favorite Terriers.

Ken's appearance caused a stir. He had just banged in the winning run and, for the time at least, was a figure of considerable importance.

"Nice goin', Ken! Some bingle!"

"That's the way to slug the old apple, boy, when the chips are down!"

The words were music to Ken's ears. They made him want to strut and throw his chest out, but he controlled the impulse. Instead, he grinned and said, "Thanks, folks. I had a little luck, that's all."

Several of them crowded in for autographs and

Ken signed score cards. He knew, of course, that if he had struck out, instead of batting in the winning run, these same fans would be leaving him severely alone. He had no illusions along those lines, but refused to let his cynicism spoil the present moment, and let the flattery engulf him.

He was glowing with well-being when the fans at last released him. There was a bounce in his stride as he started down the sidewalk. He had gone but a short way when he heard footsteps hurrying to overtake him. Probably a persistent fan with some silly question or request, he thought. He did not stop until a scratchy voice said, "Hi, Ken. How's tricks?"

Ken pulled to a halt and turned. "I'm swell, thanks. How are . . . " His throat locked tight against the words. A cold shock swept over him, freezing his thoughts into a block of solid ice.

The moment stretched into eternity, although the period probably was only a few seconds. Ken had a flash of crazy unreality, the sense of a terrible, swift journey, as if some mighty power had hurled him violently into the past. Then came the desperate urgency to bridge the gap once more, to drag himself back into the present by whatever force he could command. He fought against the shock and won, aided by the instinct of all living things to stand and fight when cornered.

He spoke and was amazed to hear his voice emerge at proper pitch. "Hi, Soapy."

"Hi, pal. I figured you'd remember me."

It was a logical assumption, because men like Soapy Barkin are not easily forgotten. He was a weasel of a person in ill-fitting, baggy clothes. His face was narrow, pinched with meanness and a sly cupidity. His lips were thin, and he wet them frequently with a darting motion of his tongue. His eyes, set close together, never rested on an object, always slid across it.

Ken asked, "What's on your mind?"

"Nothin', pal. That is, nothin' to amount to anything," said Soapy, flicking his eyes past Ken's. "I just figured it would be nice to look up one of my old pals."

"And so?" Ken prompted, feeling the chill moisture oozing to his palms.

"Oh, nothin', nothin' at all," repeated Soapy with elaborate nonchalance. "I just happened to see your picture in the paper. I noticed how good you was doing and figured maybe you'd forgot to mention you used to know guys like me." His eyes skidded across Ken's face again. "Am I right, pal?"

"And what if you are right?"

Soapy risked another quick glance at Ken's eyes, then stepped back hastily at what he saw. He gathered his courage, and when he spoke his voice emerged in a thin whine. "I'm down and out, pal. You're in the velvet. Us guys ought to stick together. How about a little loan, pal, just enough to help me along till I can get on my feet?"

"You're lucky to be on your feet right now," Ken told him tonelessly. "And if you're still here in ten seconds, you won't be on your feet."

Soapy took the hint, retreating rapidly. He stopped at a safe distance, ran his tongue across his lips, and said with scratchy venom, "Think it over, pal. I'll give you a little time. Just think it over, pal. I'll be around."

Ken started for him and Soapy turned and ran. Ken didn't follow. He watched the scurrying figure until it turned again and waved a derisive hand. There was chilly perspiration on Ken's forehead, a weakness in his knees, and a hollowness inside him. His eyes were dull when he finally wheeled and walked away.

Arriving at the apartment, Ken slumped into a chair and tried to force his mind to accurate thinking. He failed miserably. Wild, unrelated thoughts went skittering about in his brain. He could not pin any of them down.

It was his indecision that upset him most. He had always prided himself upon his ability to make decisions and to see them through. But now, faced with an ugly crisis, he could not make up his mind. He even toyed with the crazy thought of agreeing to Soapy's proposition, temporarily of course, until his plans, which were working out so well, had the chance to materialize completely. After that he could reveal his own secret to the world, thereby destroying Soapy's threat.

Blackmail! The word hit him with the force of a blow. He, Ken Holt, was actually thinking of submitting to it, of paying money for the silence of another man. A flare of anger, bright and cleansing, swept across him. He felt better when the rage had passed, knowing then that Soapy Barkin would receive no blackmail money from Ken Holt.

His thoughts cleared, and some of the desperate urgency for a swift decision was removed. He considered Soapy's character, and found comfort there.

Ken knew that Soapy would not attempt to find an honest job. If he needed money, as he claimed, he would try to get it in the only way he knew, by stealing it. There was always the chance, in this event, that he would be arrested. If that happened, he would be out of circulation long enough to suit Ken Holt.

Beezer Crane came in about that time. He stared at Ken, and asked with some concern, "What's wrong?"

"An old acquaintance looked me up."

Beezer waited for a further explanation. When it did not come, he turned away, walked over to the dresser, and began to comb his hair.

"Sorry, Beezer," said Ken gruffly.

Beezer turned and grinned. "Forget it," he said promptly. "How about some chow?"

"Okay," said Ken. "Let's go."

13

The Terriers started their western trip still leading the league. They were five games ahead of their closest rivals, the Chicago Rangers, but some of the smart baseball writers were expressing gloomy thoughts, most of them agreeing that the Terriers would be lucky to return with any lead at all.

The writers were correct. The sharp coordination of the Terriers' game began to dull. They began to win, when they did win, by closer margins. They seldom lashed out now with an old-time batting rampage.

Tobin, diagnosing the trouble correctly as overstrained nerves, did the best he could. But nothing seemed to help. The Terriers' lead was being cut down.

Ken was caught in the general slump. At least it seemed that way, and when his batting average gradually began to drop, it was assumed that Ken Holt was suffering from the same ailment that beset the other Terriers.

Ken wanted to believe it also. It would have relieved his mind tremendously had he been able to. Unhappily, he couldn't. There were other facts to face, and he faced them with a sense of shame, knowing that his worries of the moment were centered upon Ken Holt and not upon the Terriers as a baseball club. He could not erase Soapy Barkin from his mind.

It hurt his game, of course, but no one blamed him. The others had troubles of their own. They invaded the Chicago stronghold of the Rangers, and the Rangers leaped upon them gleefully. The Terriers were torn to tatters. They played four games and lost four games. They ended the series in second place, trailing the Rangers by two games.

The final game was lost through an error of the

left fielder, Hap Cross. Hap failed to stop a low line drive that should have been a single. The ball took a bad hop before scooting between Hap's legs. The hit went for a double, and a man on first came in to score the winning run.

During these weeks Zip Regan had intensified his efforts as the team's practical joker and the effect on an already tense situation was not helpful. Zip may have believed his jokes would take the minds of his teammates off their baseball worries and lighten their dark mood. On the contrary, things that had seemed funny when the Terriers were leading the league had lost their humor now.

Zip always kept a supply of props for his jokes in his locker, and he always kept the locker securely fastened to prevent tampering. On the day when the Terriers lost their fourth game to the Rangers, Zip produced a long, gaily flowered apron and presented it to Hap in the dressing room.

"Next time, Hap, you can wear this. Then all you have to do is to squat down, and nothing, not even a greased pig, can get through your legs."

Hap promptly flew into a rage. He went after Zip Regan with murder in his eye. Fuzz Bankhead and Joe Flynn grabbed him before anything happened, but the incident pulled the Terrier morale down to an all-time low.

That evening the Terriers were on their way to Boston. Ken and Beezer were sitting together in their Pullman section when Jake Tobin moved in to join them. Taking a seat opposite the two men, he said bluntly, "I need some help with Zip."

Ken and Beezer stared at him, both probably thinking the same thing—that if Jake Tobin needed help, the situation must indeed be serious. Ken found his voice first.

"How *can* we help you? We'll do anything we can, Jake. You know that."

"Yeah," said Tobin. "But it looks like a job for Beezer."

"Me?" said the astonished Beezer.

"Yes, you. He's ridden you harder than any of the others. You've weathered it fine, but I've a hunch you haven't forgotten any of it. I've also got a hunch you're a dangerous man to tangle with."

"Could be," admitted Beezer with a grin.

"Particularly," continued Tobin pointedly, "if you had my permission to shoot the works."

Beezer jerked forward in his seat. "Do you mean that?" he demanded eagerly.

"I've got to mean it," said Tobin grimly. "It's reached the point where Zip has to be slowed down and, as I see it, the only thing that'll do the trick is a dose of his own medicine, a big dose. If it's big enough he'll pull his neck in. I don't want him hurt but I want him cured. It's up to you."

Beezer's grin was beatific now. "I've been studying the problem," he admitted honestly.

"He'll be harder than a fox to trick," said Tobin.

"Oh sure, but even foxes like Zip have their weaknesses."

Tobin opened his mouth, then closed it with determination. There was a moment's silence before Tobin said anything more. "I'm not asking any questions. I don't want to know what evil thoughts are in that brain of yours." Tobin grinned. "But somehow I feel sorry for Zip Regan. I feel better now. Good night, gentlemen."

When the manager had left, Ken asked, "Got a plan, Beezer?"

"A vague one," admitted Beezer. "But no details."

"You said something about a weakness. Do you think Zip's got one?"

"I know he has."

"What?"

"Blood."

"It's a very cheerful thought but I don't get it."

"Well, it's the sort of thing you don't like to bear down on unless the situation's desperate. But Jake seems to think it is."

"And so?"

"I happened to be in the trainer's room one day when Hap Cross came in with a spike cut on his leg. It was bleeding quite a lot, all over his leg. Hap was on the table. Clem was working on the cut when I looked up and saw Zip in the doorway. Zip turned white, looked like he was going to faint, and backed out just in time. Blood affects some people like that, just like snakes used to affect me."

"I get it now. You're going to cut somebody's throat."

"No, we'll let Zip do it if it can be arranged."

"What's hard about that? Just give 'im a knife and—"

"Pipe down," said Beezer. "I want to think. I know there's an angle somewhere, and if there is I'll find it. Naturally, I'll have to fit it to suit the circumstances."

"Naturally," said Ken.

"There's one thing I'm sure of," Beezer went on,

ignoring Ken's mild irony. "Zip won't keep us waiting long."

"How can you be sure of that?"

"Because I know Zip. I've watched him work, and I think I know his system. He keeps to a sort of pattern. Once he gets under a person's hide, like he got under Hap's today, he won't let it drop. He'll pull another gag the first chance he gets."

"And your idea is to be ready for him when he pulls it?"

"Yes."

"Sounds pretty complicated to me, unless you know what he's going to pull."

"It won't be a matter of what he pulls so much as when he pulls it. I've got to depend on his following his usual system. He likes an audience, the bigger the better. A large percentage of his gags have been pulled in the locker room because he always has an audience there. That's the way I'll figure it."

"It's a pretty long chance, isn't it?"

"Not too long. Sooner or later he'll run true to form, and the point is to have the stage set for him when he does."

Ken shook his head. "It's too much for me," he admitted.

"I'll work it out," said Beezer grimly.

On the following day Beezer began to show a subdued excitement, indication that his brain was grinding out a plan that suited him. He was beaming by the time the Terriers reached Boston.

When they had checked in at their hotel, Beezer told his plan to Ken.

Listening attentively, Ken grinned with admiration. "It should work," he conceded carefully, "if you get the breaks and if Zip runs true to form."

"It's worth the gamble," Beezer said. "And now, I've got a lot of work to do. I've got to tip everybody off but Zip, and hand out the fattest parts to the best actors."

"What you need," said Ken, "is a movie director."

"It'd help," admitted Beezer. "But I'll do my best without one. I'll see Jake Tobin first and get his okay on the deal. Then we've got to be all set when Zip goes to work on Hap again. It may not be today, but it'll be soon."

"Do you think Hap can put it over?"

"He won't need to do much acting. The part'll be a natural for him."

Zip Regan was an accommodating victim. He didn't keep the Terriers waiting. He ran true to form, as Beezer Crane had prophesied.

The Terriers won the opener by a tight 3–2 decision, and when Zip Regan hurried to the dressing room ahead of the others, pleased looks of understanding passed between the Terriers.

"I think he's up to something," Beezer said. "Keep your eyes peeled." He moved to Hap Cross's shoulder for a few final words of instruction.

When the Terriers reached the dressing room, Zip Regan, a picture of innocence, was taking off his spikes. The Terriers almost overdid their air of casualness, but Zip, shooting covert glances at Hap Cross, showed no symptoms of suspicion.

Hap finally approached his locker and reached for the handle of the door with a reluctance he could not restrain, assuming that whatever surprise Zip Regan might have planned would be inside the locker.

It was. When Hap finally pulled the handle, Zip's surprise was hanging blatantly on the inside of the door. It was a fisherman's landing net, a short-handled affair for scooping in small fish. There was a red bow upon the handle of the net and a big placard reading, *To be used for grounders.*

Hap stared at it for a moment. His neck began to swell with rage and he was not acting. He whirled and started for Zip.

Things happened fast then, quite as if the whole procedure had been rehearsed. As Hap rushed toward Zip, three Terriers moved in to block Zip's view of Hap. Hap pretended to stumble, and crashed noisily against the steel lockers on his right.

When he hit the floor, he turned obediently on his back. Meanwhile Truck Hawley had reached swiftly into his locker. He had a paper cup half full of tomato catsup concealed in his big hand. He moved rapidly, dumped the catsup on Hap's upturned face, then crumpled the cup in his hand. When Hap had been properly decorated, the three men making a show of holding Zip moved aside enough for Zip to see the horrifying object on the floor.

Zip's breath rasped harshly in his throat. His eyes glazed and the color left his face. Whatever thoughts were rushing through his brain were violent. He was probably viewing his own handiwork, knowing that he was to blame. He was also fighting against his unreasoning terror at the sight of blood.

He lost the fight, adding a touch to the situation that the Terriers had not planned, but that simplified the thing a lot. He let out a gentle squeak and passed out cold.

"Great!" yelped Beezer with delight. "Better than I'd hoped. Okay, Hap."

Hap climbed to his feet and complained irritably, "Did you have to put that much stuff on me? What do you think I am, a hamburger? You forgot the onion."

Jake Tobin tossed him a towel. "Things are working out fine," he said. "Now get in the training room, Hap, while we go on with the show. Somebody throw some water on our sleeping beauty."

Ice water from the cooler soon brought Zip around. He sat dazed for a moment. When memory returned, he muttered hoarsely, "Hap! What about him? Is . . . is he . . ."

The words faded when he saw Jake Tobin backing out of the training room. Speaking to the trainer, Tobin said loudly, "You think it's a fracture, Clem? A bad one? You can't stop the bleeding?"

Tobin whirled toward the locker room and roared orders. "You, Flynn! Get the doctor in here quick! Beezer! Get on the phone fast and call an ambulance!"

Zip Regan forced himself off the bench and staggered toward Tobin, pleading, "Jake, please, I—"

Tobin spun on him and bellowed, "Shut up!

You've done enough and you've said enough! Now get out of here! Beat it, before I lose control. Go back to the hotel!"

Zip, still in his baseball uniform, started numbly toward the door, his face the color of an underdone biscuit. Tobin sent Hal Mercer to be sure Zip got away in a taxi, and when Mercer returned the Terriers settled down to enjoy themselves. Joe Flynn expressed the worried thought, "Do you think we can get him down to dinner?"

"I'll see to that," said Tobin grimly. "He'll be there. And unless I miss my guess, he'll be a pushover for the rest of it. We've got 'im half nuts as it is."

Jake Tobin kept his word, and Zip Regan came to dinner with the others. The Terriers sat at a long single table in a private dining room, and when they took their places one chair, Hap's, was glaringly unoccupied.

The Terriers were a sober, gloomy bunch, refusing to a man to meet Zip's pleading eyes. Zip himself was in a satisfactorily bad condition. His nerves were ready to crack at the slightest pressure. When he tried to eat his soup, the spoon rattled against his teeth, as dragons of remorse clawed at his soul.

The Terriers were not helpful. Fuzz Bankhead said irritably to Tobin, "Look, Jake, they must have told you *something* about his chances. Will he make it or won't he?"

"Do many people live through serious fractures?" Tobin snarled at him. "Do many people stay alive when their skulls are split wide open?"

"As bad as that, huh?" Fuzz demanded thinly.

A shiver ran along the table. A spoonful of soup spilled down Zip's shirt front.

Beezer said, "That blood just *squirted* out!"

Zip Regan came halfway erect and screamed, "Shut up! Shut up, I tell you!"

Blank faces turned in his direction. Tobin said bluntly, "Follow your own advice. Sit down and keep quiet."

Zip sank back into his chair, the strength drained out of him. But only temporarily. Suddenly, with the violence of a puppet jerked by strings, he sat bolt upright in his chair. His eyes stared wildly toward the doorway. Suddenly a great light of joy leaped to his face. He spoke hoarsely. "Hap! Hap Cross!"

The eyes of the Terriers followed the direction of Zip's stare. Hap Cross, his face glistening white with grease paint, came slowly into the room with measured tread.

The eyes of the Terriers came back to Zip, blank, puzzled eyes, conveying the impression that they hadn't seen a thing.

Zip tried again. "Hap! Hap!"

Hap took the seat reserved for him and stared with unseeing eyes straight ahead.

Zip leaped to his feet, the chair clattering to the floor behind him. He pointed a trembling finger.

"It's Hap!" he yelled. "Hap Cross! He's sitting right there! Don't you *see* him?"

The Terriers turned their heads obligingly, then looked back at Zip, apparently completely puzzled. Zip stood for a frozen, incredulous moment, fighting with his sanity.

Jake Tobin got up, looking worried. He went to Zip, put an arm around the shortstop's shoulders and said soothingly, "Take it easy, son. Just take it easy. You've had a tough experience, kid. Better go to your room now, and I'll send a doctor up."

Zip turned agonized eyes toward Tobin. "But . . . but I see him, Jake," he said through stiffened lips. "I see him!"

"Sure you do, son, sure you do. Hike along now. You'll be all right tomorrow."

Zip tried once more, but he tried with the beaten air of a frightened man who believes he has lost a fight. The words were hard to form, but he got them out. "Don't *you* see him, Jake?"

"Who, me?" said Tobin. "Of course I see him. We all see him." He called across the table. "How's your appetite, Hap?"

"Fine," said Hap. "What's holdin' up the grub?" Then he turned to Zip. "Hi, Zip. You seem upset about something. What's wrong? Don't you like my makeup? It's only grease paint."

It took Zip a short time to adjust himself. The color came back into his face and kept on coming. It finally reached the shade of violent anger as his thoughts began to click.

"A gag?" he ground out finally.

"You asked for it," said Tobin briefly.

Zip Regan had self-control and he needed it now. He came within an ace of punching Jake Tobin, but pulled himself together in time.

Finally he faced the watchful Terriers. "Jake's right. I *did* ask for it. I've been asking for it for a long time. I've known what I was doing to the team, but there was nothing I could do to stop it. Maybe it was a disease, or maybe I was just too big a jerk to try to cure it. But I think you guys have cured it. I promised myself that if Hap got well I'd never pull another gag, and I'll try to keep the promise."

He sat down and began to eat his dinner. There was some restraint around the table for a while, but gradually things returned to normal.

14

There was considerable worried speculation for the next few days as to whether or not Zip Regan's new role of good behavior would affect his baseball game. It didn't. He was as hot as ever in the field and on the bases. The Terriers relaxed and started to play baseball.

They did not attain their old-time power at once, but the improvement was encouraging. They settled down to steady playing for the remainder of their tour, and finally got back to their own park badly battered but only three games out of first place. The

St. Louis Mules, five games out of first, were tramping dangerously upon the Terriers' heels.

The Terrier fans did not receive their returning warriors with any noticeable enthusiasm. They were not in a good humor when they showed up for the opening game against the Boston Minutemen. They let it be known that they were willing to support a baseball team, but not a bunch of kiddies tossing beanbags. They were quite emphatic on the point.

The Terriers, anxious to make amends for their disastrous road trip, were in a fighting mood when they surged upon the diamond. Ken tried to share the mood, but fell far short in his attempt.

Instead of being grim and truculent, he was apprehensive, and the vagueness of his apprehension made it worse. He was afraid of something, but he didn't know quite what it was. He suffered all the absurd qualms of a small child entering a darkened room, and he hated himself for letting the sensation master him.

The game got under way at high speed. Jake Tobin selected Hank Schmidt as his starting pitcher. Schmidt was a lanky right-hander with one of the best knuckleballs in the business. Schmidt could float the ball up to the plate with all the stitches showing and with enough flutter to make it act like an apple bobbing downstream in a brook.

It was Schmidt's prize pitch, but the Minutemen behaved as if they had been trained on knuckleballs. They didn't try to bang Schmidt's offerings into the bleachers. They choked their bats, took short, hard punches, and sent a series of singles over the heads of the infielders.

Three runs piled across the plate before Tobin could warm up a relief pitcher in the bullpen. Jinks Bradshaw was finally rushed to the mound, where he finally managed to end the Boston rally. The Terriers were trailing by four runs when they took their first turn at the plate.

Zip Regan beat out a bunt, and stole second on the first pitch to Joe Flynn. Flynn grounded out to the pitcher, leaving Zip on second. The third man up, Hap Cross, got a scratch single, sending Zip to third. Cy Borg drew a walk to fill the bases.

It was a fine spot for a man to make a hero of himself, and the Terrier fans demanded it of Ken Holt when he stepped into the batter's box. Ken tried to feel like a hero. He tried to tell himself he was going to clout one out against the boards for extra bases, but the conviction would not hold.

There was a cramped tightness to his shoulder muscles. His wrists felt stiff and his throat was dry.

He took a wide pitch for a ball, realizing with a start that he had almost tried for it. Another ball, low inside, put him ahead in the count and raised his hopes.

He then took a pair of called strikes, and some of the fans began to jeer. A high fast one past the visor of his cap went for a third ball. The count was full. Ken pulled himself together for the payoff ball. It came in low, about knee-high. It might have gone for a ball, but Ken dared not take the chance.

He swung, knowing as he did so that the effort showed a touch of panic. But he connected. He even felt a satisfying jar run up his arms. As he headed for first base, he saw he had hit a lazy, looping fly to center field, an easy out.

Zip tagged up at third. He dug for home the instant the ball touched the fielder's mitt. The play was at the plate, a close one, but Zip's speed won. He slid in under the throw to make the score 4–1. Fuzz Bankhead popped out to the shortstop to retire the side.

Heading for his position in the outfield, Ken tried to console himself with the fact that although he hadn't made a hero of himself, he had at least chalked up another run batted in, which was better than striking out or hitting into a double play. It was small consolation, but it had to do.

The game moved on with increasing tension. Jinks Bradshaw kept the Minutemen controlled while the Terriers pecked away with single runs to tie the score. It was 4–4 when Boston went to bat in the top of the sixth.

Ken Holt was feeling better. He had rapped out a single in the third to bring in another run, and the hit had helped to calm his apprehension. He was slowly getting a grip on himself.

The first two Minutemen went out on grounders, and Bradshaw, facing the pitcher, succumbed to overconfidence. The pitcher hit a high-bouncing grounder over the third baseman's head. The lead-off man got a double putting men on second and third. Bradshaw kicked the dirt around a little on the mound, had a short session with the resin bag, and settled himself to face, he hoped, the final batter of the inning.

The batter swung at the first offering and got hold of it. It sounded like a dangerous blow, but the involuntary grunt of pain from the Terrier fans subsided promptly into sighs of satisfaction. The ball was heading deep, but high enough for safety, into center field.

Ken saw it leave the bat. He judged its line, then whirled and sprinted for the fence. When he turned to face the ball he saw he had figured it exactly right. There was time to spare. The ball had just begun to dip. He would not have to move to make the catch.

And then a voice—a raspy, scratching voice—roared from the stands behind him, "Four-ninety-three, eight-sixty-two!"

It probably sounded to the casual listener like an out-of-season football quarterback rehearsing signals, but it did not sound that way to Ken. To him it sounded like the crack of doom.

The numbers beat against him with an actual force that froze his mind and muscles. They were numbers the past had seared into his brain, to leave a scar time would never heal. They were prison numbers and Ken Holt had worn them on his back.

His eyes, in hypnotic helplessness, remained fastened on the ball. A section of his numbed brain screamed a warning to his muscles, urging them to action. The warning was effective to a certain point.

His hands came up to make the catch, but they reached for the descending ball too late. It struck his glove. He felt the impact, but the ball was too far from the pocket of his mitt to permit his hand to close upon it. It bounded clear and struck the ground.

Ken knew an instant of quick horror at the enormity of the fumble. He had missed an easy catch, booted it outrageously. He scrambled in panic for the ball, but his movements were vague and uncoordinated, like those of a man awakened violently from sleep.

When he finally captured the elusive ball, he neither stopped to think nor to spot the runners on the bases. He merely threw, with all the power he had, toward home. It was a stupid play, because two men had scored by the time the ball reached the infield.

Fuzz Bankhead tried to cut off the wild throw at second base, but it sailed over his head. Truck Hawley finally stopped it, but too late to keep the runner from sliding into third. The official scorer chalked a three-base error against Holt.

Ken sensed the wrath of the bleachers pouring over him, but he scarcely felt it. He was still too numb from shock. Even when Cy Borg came up and rasped, "What're you tryin' to do, bum, toss the game?" Ken merely stared at him with uncomprehending eyes.

A look of puzzlement replaced a portion of Borg's anger. He studied Ken intently for a moment, then grabbed Ken's shoulder and shook it sharply.

"What's wrong, Holt? You sick?"

The words and the heavy pressure of Borg's hand helped Ken to pull himself together. He released himself from Cy Borg's hand and said gruffly, "I'm okay."

"You'd better be," growled Borg, and headed back for his position.

The next Minuteman to face Bradshaw popped a high foul behind first base. Joe Flynn gathered it in to retire the side, but the harm was already done. The Minutemen were leading by two runs, 4–6, and Ken Holt was the man who had let the runs come in.

He wanted to escape from the park through the runway by the bullpen. Instead, he had to make the journey to the bench, the longest walk he had ever taken. He finally got there, keeping his face stiff against the bitter comments of the fans.

The Terriers eyed him with resentful curiosity but held their silence, knowing Ken's offense to be too serious for anyone to handle but Jake Tobin. Tobin motioned Ken to a place beside him on the bench and asked quietly, "What happened, Ken?"

"A case of rabbit ears, I guess."

"Try again, son. Rabbit ears are bad enough, but they don't make a guy come to pieces at the seams like you did."

"I'll be okay," Ken told him gruffly.

Tobin considered the statement carefully, then said with blunt significance, "I hope so, Ken."

The Minutemen, encouraged by their two-run gift from Ken, settled down doggedly to protect their unexpected lead. The Terriers went down in order in the sixth. Ken Holt contributed the third out. He took three mighty swings but failed to touch the ball. He whiffed disgracefully, and felt a cold lump in his stomach.

He went back with reluctance to his position in center field. The fans yelled at him, but it was the sort of thing he had learned to take without letting it upset him. What he was listening for, and hating himself for listening, was the grating voice of Soapy Barkin. It didn't come that inning.

But it came in the next, the top of the eighth. Ken had another chance at an easy running catch. As he came in on the ball, the numbers blasted at him from the crowd.

"Four-ninety-three, eight-sixty-two!"

Ken felt his muscles tighten dangerously but he held his stride and made the catch. A wave of relief swept over him. He knew what to expect now, and could brace himself for it. The little rat could yap his head off from now on, and Ken would catch all the flies that he could reach. He hammered the conviction hard into his brain.

The Minutemen held their lead. The Terriers threatened a rally in the ninth. Cy Borg singled with one out and Ken drew a walk. Then Fuzz Bankhead hit into a double play to end the game. The Terriers went down 6–4, and Ken Holt was unofficially credited with the defeat.

15

The following week was a bad one for Ken Holt. Soapy Barkin was at the bottom of it or, at least, he was the agent who kept Ken on the sizzling griddle of his own emotions.

Soapy's campaign was shrewd enough, depending largely upon the element of uncertainty. He did not shout the numbers at every opportunity, which made it worse. Ken never knew when the gritty voice would blare at him, yet he had the creepy feeling that Soapy Barkin was always in the bleachers behind center field. It meant that Ken must keep himself constantly braced. It meant that every time he chased a fly ball he must hold a little something in reserve, the mental strength to ignore the yell, in the event that it came.

The struggle began to affect his nerves, as Soapy obviously intended that it should. Ken missed a few difficult fielding chances that he believed he should have had. They were borderline chances, to be sure, and Ken was lucky that the official scorer called them hits instead of errors.

It was his batting, however, that suffered most, and that part puzzled him. The plate was out of the range of Soapy's voice, yet Ken's batting average dropped. Maybe, he decided miserably, he was trying too hard to slam the ball back in Soapy's lap. He shortened his grip on the bat and tried for singles. It was not the answer.

The Terriers were not blind or stupid. They saw what was going on and were quick to associate Ken's slump with the voice behind him out in center field, the voice that always yelled a string of numbers. The Terriers, too, decided it was not entirely a case of rabbit ears.

Ken steeled himself against the questioning stares of his teammates. The stares, in most instances, showed real concern; some showed mild contempt. Cy Borg made no attempt to hide his feelings. When he looked at Ken his eyes were filled with sultry satisfaction, as if this confirmed his early suspicions.

Jake Tobin, to Ken's surprise, made no effort to probe the problem of Ken's slump, but the expression in Tobin's eyes was not encouraging. There was a grimness about the looks he shot at Ken.

Ken weathered the changing attitude of the Terrier locker room. The thing that was really hard to endure was the thing he had to face each morning. The members of the Morning League were much too young to hide their feelings, or to try. Their reasoning was simple and direct. They knew Ken Holt was in a slump. They didn't know why and probably didn't care. They were concerned with facts, and particularly with the fact that Ken Holt, whom they regarded as invincible, was slipping.

Up to now they had not progressed beyond the stage of mild bewilderment and superficial worry. There was no deep mark upon them yet, because their interest in the Morning League was vital and intense. It was moving swiftly and would reach a tremendous climax soon. Ken Holt made arrangements for a team of New York youngsters to come down and play a picked team from the Morning League. A three-game series would decide a vague, inter-city championship of some sort. No team of big-league players ever approached a World Series with as much taut excitement as the members of the Morning League began to show while they groomed themselves for the visit of the New York Bearcats.

Ken tried to find some consolation in the feeling that the Morning League was firmly enough established to get along without him. He had fanned a spark into a flame, and the flame would continue burning after he had faded from the picture.

It was a satisfying thought but it left him lonely and a little sad, as if he had ended an important chapter of his life. He could organize other leagues, of course, but—the thought hit him with a jolt—not unless his own game showed improvement.

It didn't. It got worse. Fine lines of strain began to etch themselves about his lips and at the corners of his eyes. The situation was intolerable and he knew, with a growing sense of panic, that something had to be done about it. He also knew what should be done, but his panic increased when he thought of doing it. His thoughts were vacillating, indecisive.

He was finally forced to the alarming conclusion that his inability to make a clear decision might be a fundamental weakness in his character.

That really frightened him. The scare was big enough to force him to a conference with Jake Tobin, a conference, Ken suspected now, which should have been held months ago. When he entered Tobin's office, the manager eyed him critically for a moment, puffed a cloud of smoke, and snapped, "It's about time, Ken."

"Yeah," admitted Ken, "I guess it is."

"Sit down and take your time."

Ken tried to follow his advice. Easing himself into a chair beside the desk, he tried to arrange his thoughts to tell the story as it should be told. But his thoughts were a tangled mess. He started abruptly.

"I'm a jailbird—or, at least, I was."

Jake Tobin blew a placid smoke ring. Ken stared at him, astounded at the other's calm acceptance of the statement.

"Well?" demanded Ken impatiently.

"Well what?" said Tobin. "You expect me to be surprised. I'm not, because I've already figured it as one of the possible angles. I was almost certain of it when the guy in the bleachers started yelling numbers at you, and when I saw the way they affected you. I figured them for prison numbers, the ones you'd worn."

"Yes," Ken admitted weakly. "Yes, that's right. But—but why didn't you tell me what you'd guessed?"

"I preferred to hear you tell it," Tobin told him bluntly. "So go ahead."

Ken drew a steadying breath. "I spent two years in prison. I played around with a tough bunch of young punks out in San Francisco. They weren't seasoned criminals at the time, but some were heading in that direction. We'd been raised in the streets, with no decent outlet for our steam. We figured it was smart to be tough."

Tobin nodded. Ken continued, his voice unnatural.

"The gang worked up a grudge against a guy who owned a pool room. They went down to wreck the place. I didn't like the idea, but I went with them because I didn't have the guts to refuse. I was scared they'd call me yellow."

He hesitated a moment as the memory of that night crept up on him. He pulled himself together and went on.

"They heaved rocks through the windows of the

joint. I didn't have any, but I went through the motions to make 'em think I was a brave guy. One of the rocks hit a customer and hurt him pretty bad. The cops came. I turned an ankle trying to get away and they nabbed me. I was the only one they caught. I wouldn't squeal on the others, so they sent me up for a two-year stretch. And now you know."

"Yeah," said Tobin. "You told me some time ago that you didn't think this story would hurt the Terriers when it got out. Do you still believe that? If you do, let's hear your angle."

Ken felt a chill race up his spine, but it didn't last. His convictions were still strong, and he tried to voice them.

"Baseball," he said slowly, "is called our national game. If that is true, the baseball teams, particularly the big-league clubs, should be considered as much of a melting pot as the country itself. It means, as I see it, that everyone ought to have the chance to make good in baseball, even guys who have served prison terms. And if these guys do make good, it ought to be something for baseball to brag about—the fact that—well, I guess you could call it a good job of salvage."

"Do you still believe that?" insisted Tobin.

"Yes," Ken told him steadily.

"So do I," said Tobin. "So that's settled."

Ken let his breath escape with a sigh of relief.

"Which brings up another point," said Tobin. "If you felt that way about it, why didn't you tell me sooner? Why did you wait till that guy in the bleachers forced your hand?"

"Well, I might have told you if I'd known how you felt about it."

"What do you mean you might have told me? What other reason would you have for holding out?"

"The kids," Ken answered promptly.

"Come again."

"The ones I'm working with. I didn't want 'em to find out about it until I'd proved I could make the big-league grade. I wanted 'em to have the proof right before them that a guy with my background could reach the top."

"That makes some sense," admitted Tobin.

"But," Ken hurried on, "there was always the big chance I wouldn't make the grade. If I'd faded out in the first couple of months, and if the newspapers had broadcast my background, a lot of folks would have been bound to think it was because of the way I'd had to live when I was a kid, that I simply didn't have the stuff when the chips were down. And some of these gutterbred kids, even though they like baseball, would certainly have figured. 'Aw, what's the use?' "

He stopped for breath. Tobin nodded and said, "I follow you that far. Go ahead."

"But," continued Ken, trying to get his point across, "once I had made the grade, once I had finished a successful season with the Terriers, then I'd have the best argument in the world to lay before the kids. They'd know, then, that there was a chance for them to make the grade, too."

He stopped and waited anxiously. Tobin smoked for several thoughtful moments.

"You build a good case, Ken. I could find flaws in it, of course, but for the most part I follow your reasoning. The point is, however, that the thing has backfired on you. You should have told me sooner."

"Maybe," conceded Ken. Then he added doggedly, "But I thought I had it figured right. I took a chance, that's all."

"And lost?"

"No," said Ken with a flash of anger. "I haven't

lost. I've built the Morning League. It'll last, even when I'm gone."

"Going somewhere?" Tobin demanded pointedly.

Ken's head jerked up to meet the inscrutable look in the manager's eyes. Tobin shrugged and said, "We'll skip that part. But now that the Morning League is settled, had you considered giving a little thought to the Terriers?"

Ken stared at him. "I don't quite get it."

"No," said Tobin grimly. "I'm afraid you don't."

"I'm having a slump, that's all. I'll soon be out of it."

"Do you mean that now you've got this business off your chest, your game will pull itself together?"

"I guess that's what I mean."

"I hope so, Ken. And, oh yes, another thing. How did I happen to forget this? Where did you learn that brand of baseball?"

"I'd played a little sand-lot stuff before, and when I got in prison I found baseball to be the main sport. I played almost steadily for two years."

"Maybe so," said Tobin skeptically. "But no one learns to swing a bat like that against prison pitching."

Ken forced a grin and demanded, "Ever hear of Ozzie Klein?"

"Ozzie Klein?" repeated Tobin, coming forward in his chair. "Who hasn't? He was one of the greatest southpaws ever on a mound, until it went to his head and he began gambling away more than he earned. When he finally forged a check out on the coast, he—" Tobin stopped abruptly as understanding came into his eyes. "Ha-a-ay," he breathed. "Do you mean to tell me Ozzie Klein was in the same prison you were in?"

"He was there."

"And you batted against *him*?"

"Almost every day."

"Well," said Tobin, as if a great mystery had been solved. "No wonder you could clout 'em."

Ken did not miss the past tense of the verb. He said truculently, "And I'll clout 'em again."

"Yes," admitted Tobin, "I think you will. The point is—when?"

"Any day now."

"Good." Tobin changed the subject. "I'll have to tell Tom Barstow what you've told me."

Ken stiffened involuntarily, even though he had known that Barstow would have to be informed.

Thomas Barstow was the Baseball Commissioner, the high court from which all final decisions must descend.

Tobin, noticing Ken's quick concern, said reassuringly, "Don't worry. I've known Tom for a long time, and he looks at baseball the same way you and I do. He also thinks that everyone should have a chance to play the game. I'll phone his office in New York. He'll be sore because you didn't tell us sooner, but he won't make trouble for you. Take my word for it."

Ken was glad to. It was another big load off his mind.

"Will it be all right if I break it to the papers?" he asked. "Duke Gallup's been pretty good to me, and I'd like to give him a scoop."

"Suits me."

"I'd also like to tell the Terriers myself."

"Good idea," said Tobin.

Ken left the office and went back to the apartment. He was glad to find Beezer there. Ken said, "I've just spilled the works to Tobin."

"What works?" asked Beezer, puzzled.

"About where I came from before I joined the Terriers."

"Okay, I'll bite," said Beezer. "Where were you?"

Ken repeated what he had told Tobin, and Beezer accepted the story very much as the manager had accepted it, without surprise or obvious concern.

"So what?" he said. "So you were in prison. I suspected it all along. Right from the start I've pegged you for a criminal type. I guess you noticed that I've never left anything valuable lying around where you could get your hooks on it."

"Okay, okay," said Ken. "I just thought you ought to know." He started for the phone, explaining, "I'm going to tell Duke Gallup now."

He was looking up the number in the telephone directory when a knock sounded on the door. Beezer yelled, "Come in!"

The door opened cautiously, and a small figure slid around its edge. Ken turned, stiffened in his seat, then came slowly to his feet. His voice was brittle as he said, "Well, Soapy?"

Beezer showed quick interest. "So *this* is the little animal?"

"This is it," said Ken. "We were in stir together."

Soapy, his hand still on the knob of the open door, said scratchily, "Relax, Ken. Just thought we'd better talk a little business. Maybe your pal'd like to take a little walk."

Ken's first feeling was sheer amazement that

Soapy Barkin, rodent that he was, had found the courage to come here. It showed, beyond a doubt, that Soapy's confidence was huge, that he had convinced himself of his own power over Ken.

Ken's wonder passed, as rage moved in with violent force. He reached Soapy in a few swift strides, frustrating his panicky attempt to flee. Ken kicked the door closed, flashed a big right hand to the slack of Soapy's coat, and pinned him savagely against the door.

Dry cluckings came from Soapy's throat. His tongue was too paralyzed with fright to form his pleas for mercy into words. His face was olive-green with terror.

"Easy, Ken!" snapped Beezer.

The warning brought Ken to his senses. He remembered that Soapy was too small a man for him to maul. However, he retained his grip on Soapy's coat, dragging him from the door, and slamming him hard into the chair.

"Stay there, and don't move!" said Ken.

Soapy's jaw flapped, but the words of acquiescence would not come. Ken turned away and stepped back to the phone. He dialed the *Daily Sentinel* and soon had Gallup on the phone.

"Hi, Duke. This is Ken Holt."

" 'Morning, Ken. What gives?"

"I've got a scoop for you. I was a jailbird out in California before I came with the Terriers."

Ken heard a grunt at the other end as if someone had hit Duke Gallup in the solar plexus.

"Who're ya kiddin'?" Duke finally asked feebly.

"You're getting it straight, Duke, and I want you to make a story of it."

There was a long silence, so long that Ken asked, "Well?"

"Okay, Ken," said Duke at last. "You served some time. So what? You're a baseball player now. Why not forget the rest of it?"

"Are you nuts?"

"I must be," said Duke irritably. "Nobody but a half-wit would turn down as big a story as that. I'm simply advising you to let it ride."

"Thanks, Duke," said Ken quietly. "You're a good guy, and I'm grateful. But the story has to break, and I'd rather give it to you than to anyone else."

"Okay, kid," said Duke resignedly, "and thanks for the scoop. Hold on a minute till I light a cigarette. Okay, shoot. Let's have the story."

Ken gave it to him. When he had finished, he turned back to the waiting Soapy, who had begun to get his color back. However, there was venom in his eyes at the knowledge that Ken was no longer available for blackmail.

Ken said, "Scram!" and Soapy wasted no time in departing.

Beezer asked, "Feel better, Ken?"

"I . . . guess so," said Ken uncertainly. "At least, I feel as if I'd just squirmed out from under a load of bricks. That's some help, but I sure wish I knew where I was heading from here on."

"Quit worrying."

"Oh, sure. Just turn it on and off like an electric switch. I've got to break it to the Terriers before they read it in Duke's column."

"Good idea."

But not an easy one. Ken found he had never tackled a much harder job. When the club was gathered in the locker room before game time, Ken forced himself upon his feet, and said in a loud voice, "I've got something to tell you guys."

An abrupt silence settled on the room, as the Terriers turned their eyes on Ken. The expression in the eyes was varied. Some were wide with startled curiosity, some were narrowed with a quick alertness. It was evident from the different expressions that the Terriers felt Ken had been acting strangely of late, and they were prepared for almost anything.

Ken hauled in a deep breath and said, "It's time you fellows knew I served a stretch in prison before I hooked up with the Terriers. That's where I learned baseball."

Well, it was out! The walls did not collapse about Ken's ears. He searched for shocked, astounded looks and did not find them. The Terriers, for the most part, wore expressions of surprise and mild embarrassment, as if they felt called upon to comment on Ken's news and did not know what to say.

The silence hung like an uneasy cloud. Truck Hawley, the big catcher, finally spoke. "Is that the reason you've been off your game?"

"I . . . I guess so," Ken admitted.

"Huh," Truck grunted. He shot a look about him, found he had the center of the stage, and did not seem to enjoy it. The Terriers were gladly leaving the matter to him. He cleared his throat and plowed ahead.

"It looks to me," he said gruffly, "like it all boils down to this: we don't care what you did before you signed up with the Terriers. We're baseball players. It's our business, our bread and butter. The only way we want to judge a man is how he affects our business and how he behaves himself while he's around us. That's important. What he did before we knew him isn't important. If he plays ball with us, we'll play ball with him. See what I'm drivin' at?"

"Yeah," said Ken, feeling like a grammar school student being lectured by the principal.

"Okay," said Truck. "You got somethin' off your chest. It took guts to do it. We admire that part. But the part we'll admire most is to see you settle down and play the kind of baseball you started the season with. Think you can?"

"I think so."

"School dismissed," grinned Truck.

The Terriers continued with their dressing. Ken, his mind slightly dazed, was trying to decide whether he felt better or whether he didn't. He finally decided that he did. He had a big load off his conscience and that should lighten any man's spirits. Ken wondered why his spirits were not a whole lot lighter than they were.

He soon found the answer—the Morning League. The Terriers had taken the matter in their stride.

Their attitude toward Ken had not been materially affected, because, as Truck had pointed out, Ken's chief importance to the Terriers was his ability to play baseball. It was the yardstick by which they judged him, and their reaction was entirely logical.

But how would the news affect the youngsters? How would they react to the disclosure that he had been a convict? Ken was afraid he knew how they would feel about it, and the knowledge sent quivers of worry through his nerves.

He was afraid that the youngsters, because of their environment, might regard his two years in the penitentiary as something glamorous. If only he could have kept them from knowing until his position as a baseball player were secure. Then his influence over them would have been great enough so that he could tell them his own story and make the effect he wanted to produce. Then he could have made it plain, without preaching, that a jail sentence was nothing to be proud of, to put it mildly, and in his own case the effect of it might have ruined his chances in baseball. And that, Ken realized, was just the trouble. He was not at all certain that was not precisely what had happened. His future with the Terriers was anything but secure.

The worry dulled his batting eye and destroyed

16

Duke Gallup's story in the *Sentinel* was fairly written. The fact was revealed, of course, that Ken had served a prison term, but Gallup went to great pains to point out that he had more than rehabilitated himself in society. Ken was grateful for the moderation of the article.

The youngsters were all acquainted with the facts when Ken arrived next day. Their eyes told him.

Butch Browski asked with youthful lack of tact, "How'd it happen, Mr. Holt?"

"How did what happen?"

"You know, what was in the paper. About the stretch you served."

This was going to be difficult, but Ken knew he would have to face it. The youngsters were all grouped about him, waiting.

"It happened because I was a stupid young punk. Because I was scared of honest work, and because I figured the half-wits I ran around with were smart guys."

"And they were dopes?" asked Butch.

"We were all dopes to think we could make our own laws. We believed we could get away with it. I didn't. The cops nabbed me."

There were looks of sympathetic understanding in the youngsters' eyes, and Ken knew that they were not impressed by the fact that he had broken the law, but were sympathetic because he had been unlucky enough to get caught. There was a difference.

Ken tried to explain the difference to them, but their nods were perfunctory and their attention soon began to wander. They were bored, and Ken came to the slow conviction that he was making a fool of himself. His flow of fatherly advice ended abruptly.

The Busters went gratefully back to baseball, and Ken tried to reason out what had happened. He felt like a person who, when about to complete a jigsaw puzzle, had clumsily upset the thing and scattered all the parts upon the floor.

He was forced to accept the fact that his experience as a convict left the youngsters entirely unimpressed. They had seen the older members of their community go to jail and come out of jail. Their reaction was, "So what?" He had tried to lecture them, pointing out as tactfully as possible the difference between right and wrong, but he might as well have lectured them in Latin. His own status, in their eyes, remained unchanged. He was relieved but felt, somehow, as if the youngsters should have shown more active interest in his problem.

Baseball, however, was commanding their entire attention, an interest that rose to fever pitch as the date of the series against the New York Bearcats came nearer.

Ken should have been pleased at this, and he was. But he could not conquer the forlorn conviction that his efforts here were finished. The youngsters no longer needed him. He had done everything he could for them. It was time to move along to other fields, to organize another league in another district.

Then he was jolted by the realization that his own baseball would have to show considerable improvement if his work with boys were to continue at all. Unless he came out of his batting slump, he would never organize another league. His first problem was to get his eye on the ball again. That ought to be a simple matter, Ken felt. But it was not. His batting touch would not come back.

The Terrier fans received the news of his prison term with no more than a mild flurry of interest. They, like the Terriers themselves, were concerned chiefly with Ken's baseball. When he continued in his slump, their yells of anger were not against Ken Holt, the ex-convict, but against Ken Holt, the ex-baseball player.

Ken tried to change his batting stance, his grip, his swing—it was all sheer waste of time. A desperate tightness crept into his muscles and a creeping panic took control of them. It was not unusual now for Ken to spend a game upon the bench, the sure sign that a player is slipping.

Beezer was almost as concerned about it as Ken himself. The two men spent numerous gloomy sessions swapping theories and trying to devise a cure. One day Beezer asked, "May I be frank?"

"Why not? Shoot."

"You don't seem to have any real incentive to play baseball anymore."

"I've got plenty of incentive," Ken said gruffly.

"Not the sort you need. When you hooked up with the Terriers, you had the incentive of overcoming your background. It was a dumb idea, but it seemed important to you and it kept you going. Right?"

"Have it your own way," said Ken ungraciously.

"You also had the kids. The Morning League was a big shot in the arm for you. Now you figure the kids don't need you anymore."

"Maybe," Ken admitted reluctantly. "But I want to organize more leagues. That ought to be enough incentive to put me back on my game."

"Apparently it isn't. Now I'll tell you what I really think. I think you need a good kick in the pants to make you forget all about Ken Holt for a while."

Ken did not reply.

The Terriers had battled themselves into the lead again, a slim lead, to be sure, but they were holding grimly to it, unaided by Ken's bat. The Rangers were snorting at the Terriers's heels and Jake Tobin showed the strain. He had done his best to help

Ken Holt regain his batting form, but his best was not good enough.

The Rangers came roaring into the homestretch of the season as if they were jet-propelled. They boosted the Terriers out of first place by a half-game margin. And that is how matters stood when the Rangers invaded Philadelphia for a final three-game series, the winner of which would emerge with the pennant safely tucked away, and would move on to the dizzy heights of World Series competition.

The Terriers, facing the colossal opportunity, were taut as violin strings. They were all resentful now of the one weak spot in the lineup—Ken Holt.

Ken accepted the resentment with resigned helplessness. He did not blame his teammates. He had started as a brilliant rookie and had completely fizzled out. He did not know quite how the thing had happened, but it had. The handwriting on the wall was all too clear, and when the ax fell Ken was not taken completely by surprise.

It fell on the morning of the first game of the Terrier-Ranger series. Ken feared the worst as he obeyed a summons to Jake Tobin's office, and his fears were confirmed by the first glance at the manager's face. It wore the set expression of a man about to perform an unpleasant task.

"It's bad news, Ken," he said without preamble.

Ken, keeping his own face blank, said, "I guess I've been expecting it."

Tobin passed a gnarled hand across his head in a gesture of frustration. Finally he exploded. "Blast it, Ken! I'm not doing this because I want to! I think it's a filthy trick to let you out this late in the season. But after all, I don't own this outfit. These are orders from the top."

Ken made a dismal guess. "Sold down the river?"

"Well, it's not quite as bad as that. We're farming you out to one of our own clubs, the Badgers. It's only a matter of giving you the chance to find yourself again and to get your feet back on the ground. I'm sorry, Ken."

Ken hauled in a long, slow breath. "Yeah, Jake," he said. "I'm sorry, too. Sorry I let you down. How much time have I got left?"

"Three days," Tobin told him gruffly. "Time enough to see our series with the Rangers."

"That's good," said Ken. "I can also watch my kids play their first game against the Bearcats. Their series starts day after tomorrow. It'll make it easier for me to leave if I can see 'em win their first game, anyway."

Tobin studied him intently, a hardness creeping

into his eyes. "How about seeing the Terriers win?" he demanded bluntly. "Wouldn't that help, too?"

"Oh sure," Ken answered hastily. "Sure it would."

Tobin leaned back in his chair and stared at Ken. The expression in his eyes was not complimentary. He said finally, "I guess that sews it up. I've suspected it for some time, but I *know* now why you missed the boat."

Ken stared back at Tobin. "I . . . I don't get it," he blurted.

"Naturally you don't," said Tobin, "or you probably would have tried to cure it. But here it is, Ken, as I see it: you've been playing baseball for the kids, not for the Terriers."

Ken started a quick protest, but Tobin cut him short. "Don't get me wrong. I think you've done a whale of a job with those youngsters, and you've got plenty to be proud of. But the point is, Ken, that you've never really become one of the cogs in the Terrier machine."

"It doesn't make sense," said Ken.

"It makes lots of sense," said Tobin sharply. "I'm sure it's true. When you started to go to pieces, you had nothing to fall back on. The Terriers would have been glad to help, but you couldn't fall back on them because you never made yourself one of the club. And when the pinch came, you didn't have their confidence behind you. You've got to believe in a club, Ken, before you can give your best to it."

Ken's thoughts were still fumbling in confusion. He admitted finally, "You . . . you could be right, I guess. But what can I do about it now?"

Tobin shrugged his shoulders. "I don't know. It's something you'll have to learn while you're with the Badgers."

Ken started toward the door. Then, as a bad thought struck him, he turned to face the manager again. "I guess this stuff'll all be in the papers."

"I don't think so," Tobin said. "I'm keeping it from the papers until you leave, and I've asked the Badger manager to do the same."

"Thanks, Jake. So long."

Ken spent the next morning with the Busters, but they were too excited over the coming visit of the Bearcats to notice his depression.

In the afternoon, he sat listlessly on the bench while the Terriers played the Rangers. It was a terrific ball game, ending in a nerve-racking 3–2 victory for the Terriers.

The second game was sheer disaster. The Rangers showed the relentless power they had developed in the past few weeks. Their batters plastered the outfield wall with hits. It was more of a track meet than a ball game. The final score was 10–1.

It was a stiff dose of poison for the Terriers and their fans to take. The Terriers were numb with shock as they headed for the dressing room, and when the numbness gave way to reality they were hard-eyed, desperate, frankly scared.

Ken, unnoticed in the dressing room, began to feel a strange sensation creeping over him. He had had it before, vaguely, but now it rushed upon him with full force. It was a feeling of utter loneliness, of complete, unqualified exclusion. He began to understand what Tobin had implied by saying he was not one of the Terriers, and the understanding was not pleasant.

It was emphasized by his close association with Beezer Crane. Beezer was a Terrier. Ken wasn't. The gap was there and probably would widen. He had not told Beezer of his release.

They were sitting in their apartment on the evening of the Ranger triumph. Beezer, as if trying to torture himself further, was gloomily reading the sport page of the evening paper. Suddenly he stiffened in his chair.

"What's this!" he gasped.

"What's what?" asked Ken perfunctorily.

"The Terriers have farmed you to the Badgers!" Beezer was aghast. "Why didn't you tell me?"

"I . . . I intended to," Ken told him dully. "But I . . . well, I wanted to put it off as long as possible."

Beezer's face was twisted with concern. Then he stared at Ken and said, "You look as if you'd only just heard the news."

"No, I'd heard it. Tobin told me. It's just that I didn't expect the papers to get hold of it, not yet. Tobin tried to keep it dark, but there must have been a leak at the other end."

Beezer thought this over carefully. "You didn't want the kids to know."

"I guess I didn't. They're playing their first game with the New York kids tomorrow. I've got to be there, of course, but it'll be tough to face 'em."

"I suppose it will." Then, after a moment's silence, Beezer said, "I'd sort of like to see that game myself."

Ken shot him a grateful look. He was offering his moral support, an understanding gesture which Ken appreciated deeply.

"Thanks, Beezer. I'd like to have you there. You know that. But it's the sort of thing I've got to face alone."

"Sure," said Beezer in complete agreement. "I'll keep my fingers crossed. That'll keep the whammy off."

"I hope so," Ken said fervently.

17

Ken did not get much sleep that night. He was tortured by long periods of rigid wakefulness. He was drawn and haggard in the morning, and when he approached the ball field where the Bearcats and the Busters would meet, his stride was stiff and lifeless.

Seeing his approach, Nick Browski came to meet him, his hard young face set in worried lines.

"Tough luck, Ken," he said. "I'm sorry."

"Do they know?" asked Ken, nodding toward the diamond.

"Yeah, they know."

"How're they taking it?"

Nick lifted his shoulders in a puzzled gesture. "I'll be darned if I can figure it out," he said. "They act sort of punch-drunk."

It was not very helpful information, but when Ken forced himself to cover the final distance to the diamond, he learned that Nick's description of the Busters' behavior was as accurate as any he could have devised himself.

They were displaying a mild form of hysteria. They seemed to be trying frantically to maintain their confidence in spite of a shock they had no way of understanding.

This was borne out in their attitude toward Ken. They knew he had been dropped from the Terriers, but no accusation or resentment showed in their eyes. They were badly befuddled.

When the game got under way, they played with a crazy desperation that destroyed their coordination. They played like a team that accepted the fact that it had a tremendous handicap to overcome, something nameless but entirely sinister.

Ken watched them from the bench. He saw them take a beating they never should have taken, because his experienced eyes assured him beyond doubt that the Busters, man for man, were far superior to the Bearcats. Yet the Bearcats made the hometeam look like beginners.

Another expression showed on their faces now, between innings, when they came to the players' bench where Ken Holt sat. The looks they shot in his direction were accusing, as if they finally understood that he had let them down.

Ken saw all this. He saw his team outclassed and thrashed. He was sorry for the youngsters, but the sorrow was only a ripple on the flood of his emotions.

He heard Nick Browski, sitting on the bench beside him, growl, "They didn't have a chance."

Ken turned his head toward Nick. Nick looked at Ken and his eyes were ugly.

"And *you* know why," Nick said.

"I guess I do."

"You let 'em down."

"I'm beginning to understand that now."

"*Beginning* to understand it?" Nick shot at him. "What do you mean, beginning? Are you stupid?"

"Yeah," said Ken. "I was. I figured the kids could get along without me. I didn't think they'd need me any longer."

Nick stared at him incredulously. Some of his

anger was dissolved by wonder. "Are you nuts?" he demanded harshly.

"That's the way I had it figured. But the kids do need me." There was a touch of awe in Ken Holt's voice.

"Of course they need you," Nick declared with a helpless exasperation. "They need you in this series, at any rate, not the way you are but the way you were. Holy cats, man! They figured you and baseball as the same thing. They had you up there like a little tin god. And when you collapsed, got kicked off the Terriers, the kids collapsed too, and they don't know why. They'll get over it, sure, but not right away, not in time to take the Bearcats."

Thoughts were churning in Ken's mind, but they began to take form fast. The thing that hit him hardest was a raging anger at himself. He had guessed wrong all the way down the line. He had left a job half done. In fact, there was no job he had succeeded in doing right.

He got to his feet and said to Nick, "Our kids can lick the Bearcats if our kids are right. They've got to be right, Nick, for the next two games."

"Oh sure," said Nick sardonically. "Just like that."

"Could be."

"Are you kiddin'?"

"I hope not. I'm leaving now, because there's nothing I can do to save the kids today." He started away, then turned back as an idea hit him. "Bring the Busters to the game this afternoon," he said. "I'll have a block of twenty tickets for you at the bleacher gate."

"Okay," said Nick. "We'll be there."

Ken started for the Terrier park. He cooled off enough on the way to wonder whether he was making still more of a fool of himself. He had enough determination left, however, to walk into Tobin's office. The manager, luckily, was there. He eyed Ken with quick interest.

"What's eating you?" he demanded.

"I want to play this afternoon."

Tobin choked on a mouthful of cigar smoke. He coughed, pulled out a handkerchief, and wiped his eyes. When he removed the handkerchief, his expression was unreadable.

"You probably do. But do you know any good reason why I should put you in?"

"It may not sound good to you," admitted Ken, "but seems all right to me. Both you and Beezer have said things to me in the last few days, different things, but they tie together. Also I've done some thinking."

"Let's hear about it."

"Okay," said Ken. "Here it is."

He related what had happened at the game he had just attended. He spoke carefully, trying to make his feelings clear, trying to convince Tobin that his confidence was back because of his realization that the kids needed him.

"And is that enough," demanded Tobin pointedly, "to make you clout the apple?"

"It's a start," said Ken. "The rest is a little vague, but when I saw the kids booting the ball around today it struck me how important it was to have confidence in the other guys around you on the field. The kids' confidence was all tied up in *me*. I let 'em down and they collapsed. If I get another chance, I'll build their confidence around the team."

Tobin nodded and said, "Go on."

"It struck me then that I'd been doing the same thing here. My biggest interest in the Terriers was in using them as a means toward an end. I was playing baseball for myself. If it had been the other way, I might still be on the team."

"Sure," said Tobin. "But are you trying to tell me that your change of heart can make you play a good game?"

"No," said Ken with a flash of anger. "How do I know that? But I can try from a different angle."

"Well," said Tobin flatly, "the big point is that you're asking me to take a big chance, Ken, to stick my neck out a long, long way. Would you do it if you were in my shoes?"

"I probably would, if I knew as much about ball players as you're supposed to."

Tobin studied Ken intently, his eyes boring steadily into those of the younger man. Ken withstood the pressure grimly, keeping his own eyes level.

"I'm a fool," the manager said at last. "An old soft-headed fool. There *have* been cases of men snapping out of a slump overnight. You'll start in center field this afternoon."

Ken felt the blood pound hard against his temples, but he kept his face impassive.

"Thanks," he said. "I promised the kids a block of twenty bleacher seats. Can you fix it up?"

Tobin shifted his cigar and glowered. "You're really pushing me around, aren't you?"

"I'm doing my best," conceded Ken.

"I'll make 'em grandstand seats," growled Tobin. "I might as well be a colossal fool as an ordinary one."

"Thanks, Jake."

"Get out! I've got some worryin' to do."

Ken also had worrying to do. He understood in a very definite way that he had never had more to worry about in his entire life. Yet he realized with surprise that he was actually anticipating the game a few hours hence. He was looking forward to it with the hunger of a man who has been living on a diet of bread and water and is presented with a big porterhouse steak. There was life in his muscles and an amazing calmness in his soul.

Ken knew he had his back against the wall. He was facing his last fight for survival. It was win or lose. He was experiencing, in a way, the tranquility of desperation, a sort of gratitude that all uncertainty would soon be over.

He explained this to Beezer Crane as they headed for the ballpark. Beezer listened carefully and said, "You're nuts."

"Maybe," Ken admitted mildly, "but it's a peaceful sort of nuttiness."

"Sure, but I think you're hidin' your head in a hole like an ostrich."

"So?"

"Yeah, so."

"Okay, wise guy, sound off."

"It'll sound corny to you, but here it is. When you got dropped from the club, it dawned on you you'd missed something. Maybe you even figured it out that you might have given the guys on the club a lot you didn't give 'em. Maybe you've got a different idea of the whole setup."

There was a long silence. Ken finally admitted quietly, "I guess I have." Then he added with gruff embarrassment, "It's a good feeling."

"Keep your hooks in it and you'll play baseball."

18

Ken's eagerness to rejoin the Terriers was not reflected by the Terriers themselves. That was perfectly evident when Ken reached the dressing room. Most of the men were there, and the quick silence that Ken's entrance caused was full of significance. They had heard, undoubtedly, that Ken would play against the Rangers.

The glances shot his way were openly resentful. Some Terriers let their eyes rest on him longer than the others, and then their expressions changed to astonishment, caused by Ken's new air of ease and confidence. He was no longer poker-faced and haggard. There was a new look in his eyes and a new spring to his stride.

Cy Borg was an exception. He stared hard at Ken and did not change his expression. Borg's eyes were hot with outrage, but he held his wrath until Jake Tobin entered. Then Borg exploded.

"Are you crazy, Jake?" he yelled. "We've got to win this game! You can't put that busher back in center field to gum the works!"

Jake Tobin turned upon him slowly. The manager's face was drawn with worry and responsibility, but his eyes were hard. He spoke in a gentle, normal tone of voice. "I've got a spot on the bench for players who don't like the way I run things. Just one more word, Cy, and you'll warm that spot."

Cy's face took on a strangled look as he choked upon the words already near the surface. But he held them back.

Tobin turned upon the others. "Any suggestions from you men?" he inquired.

There were none. They turned grimly to their dressing, visibly affected by Borg's blow-off. Whatever temporary confidence they had felt in Ken was gone.

Batting practice did not prove much to Ken. He hit the ball as well as any of the rest, but even in the worst of his recent days it had always been like that. He had been able to relax against the easy deliveries of his own practice hurlers.

In fielding practice he chased fungos, catching some hard ones, which didn't prove much either. His fielding had never suffered to any great extent, being less dependent than batting upon split-second timing.

He waited for his presence in the lineup to bring forth a blast of protests from the fans, but there were only a few. The fans, because of yesterday's defeat, were willing to put their faith in Tobin's masterminding in a crisis such as this.

Tension, however, had mounted to a fever pitch when the umpire finally yelled, "Play ball!" The fans had worked themselves into a hopeful frenzy, knowing that this game would decide the pennant. The Terriers were tight-lipped. The Rangers were cocky and assured.

Bunker went to the mound for the Terriers to open the top of the first inning. Bunker was a big right-hander, an uneven pitcher. On his good days he was marvelous, and Ken hoped this was one of them with an intensity that made him realize how desperately he wanted the Terriers to win. It was a new feeling and he felt its warmth go surging through his veins. He liked it.

The first Ranger whacked a snappy grounder to Zip Regan, but Zip scooped it up and the man was out at first.

Bunker coaxed the second Ranger into a couple of fast strikes, then felt him out with a pair of wide ones to make the count two and two. The Ranger hit the fifth pitch for a single into center field. Ken fielded the ball smoothly on the second bounce, and held the runner at first.

The third man up flied out to left field. The fourth laid down a surprise bunt along the first-base line. He came within an ace of beating it out, but Bunker, a good fielding pitcher, came off the mound fast, snatched up the ball, and flipped it to Joe Flynn at first. The first-base umpire called the runner out.

The Terriers were grim as they took their turn at the plate in the last of the first. They were facing Sam Dillon, a rangy southpaw who could be mighty annoying at times. He had a season record of nine wins and six defeats, and he did not seem worried about the Terrier bats.

Zip Regan, lead-off man, hit the first pitch and sent a whooping grounder down toward third. It looked as if it might get through, but the Ranger third baseman made a brilliant stop, came up with the ball, and lined it to first base for the out.

Joe Flynn, the next batter, had better luck. He sent a grounder between first and second for a neat single. Hap Cross also got a short single to left field, putting runners on first and second with one out.

It was Cy Borg's chance to make a hero of himself early in the game. He strode toward the plate, glancing at Ken Holt who was selecting his bat from the rack. The look said, "I'll clear the bases so the Terriers won't have to depend on *you*."

Borg took a ball, then swung on the second offering with force enough to brain an elephant. The slow curve fooled him. His bat disturbed nothing but the air, while the force of his swing sent him down on one knee.

He settled himself once more in the batter's box. He took another ball, then swung mightily at the fourth pitch but overcut it badly. The ball reached the shortstop on one fast bounce. The shortstop tossed it to the second baseman who covered the bag and rifled the ball to first base for the double play. The Terriers had lost their scoring chance.

In the top of the second, Bunker began to look as if this were certainly one of his good days, setting the three Rangers down in order. Ken watched with approval but with mounting tenseness, knowing he would be the lead-off Terrier in the bottom of the second inning.

The tension increased as he approached the dugout. The Terriers, converging there, began to shoot quick looks at him, as if it were vitally important for them to know just what was going on inside him, because a portion of their fate had been entrusted to his hands. There was uncertainty in their glances, too, as if they felt they should do something but didn't quite know what.

Zip Regan solved the problem. He may have done it through deliberate reasoning or it may have been instinct. Ken Holt was at the bat rack, picking out his bat. The Terriers were in the dugout on the bench.

Zip Regan yelped, "Get out there, Ken, and start us off!"

Ken's muscles twitched from the unexpected impact of the words. They came as a complete surprise, caught him with his guard down. His quick side glance of gratitude was involuntary, uncontrolled. It may have tipped the balance with the others, because a flood of words came snapping at him from the dugout.

"Pin that southpaw's ears back, Ken!"

"Give it a ride, kid!"

"Lose the old apple, fella! Give it to the bleachers!"

Ken felt a foolish tightness in his throat, an embarrassing mist before his eyes. He headed for the plate, glad for the moment's delay while the Ranger catcher climbed into his tools and the umpire dusted off the plate.

The Terriers back there on the bench had told him he was a member of the club. Perhaps their honest opinions of Ken Holt were low, but he wore a Terrier uniform and was about to go to bat for them. It was a moment of high crisis, this game against the Rangers, and the Terriers would not permit themselves to doubt even the questionable ability of Ken Holt.

It was the sort of thing, Ken understood now, that made a ball club great. It had probably been going on before his eyes for months and he had been blind to it. But now, however limited the time might be, Ken Holt was a Terrier. The other members of the club, excluding Borg, had told him so.

The umpire said, "Let's go."

Ken stepped into the batter's box. His feet instinctively assumed the old-time reaching stance; he forgot that recently he had been experimenting with a closer one. He jerked at the visor of his cap, a gesture filled with challenge that Sam Dillon recognized.

He studied Ken Holt carefully. He had heard of Ken's bad slump, but there was nothing about him now that suggested a lack of confidence. Dillon was puzzled, but he was a clever pitcher. He threw one in, keeping it low. Ken ignored it. Ball one.

The next delivery came in high, outside. Ken let it go. Ball two. Then Dillon tried to hook the next one over. Ken almost went for it but not quite. The umpire called another ball. Ken's batting eye was back to normal. He had the pitcher in a hole.

The next pitch should be an automatic take, but Ken was not taking anything for granted. He flicked a glance at Tobin, who was coaching at first base. Ken got a quick shock of surprise and gratitude when Tobin flashed him the hit sign.

Tobin was in there fighting with him. He was taking a small gamble in order to give Ken a break, figuring that the next pitch would be right through the plate and that Ken should have an easy chance to meet it.

Ken figured it that way too, until his eyes went back to Dillon. Then he got the impression that Dillon knew the batter had been ordered to hit the next one. Maybe some smart Ranger had stolen Tobin's sign and flashed it back to Dillon. Ken's impression was strengthened when Dillon shook off the catcher's sign, then nodded when he had the one he wanted.

So Ken was not expecting a fireball over the heart of the plate. That was just as well, because Sam Dillon's next pitch was a fast-breaking hook, chest high.

Ken watched it all the way. His swing was loose and free, his wrist-snap like a golfer's. When the solid jar of contact traveled up his arms, Ken knew the ball had been really hit.

It should have been a double, but the left field wall was tricky and the fielder was unfamiliar with it. Ken ended up at third, and the Terrier fans went crazy.

So did the Terriers themselves. They cavorted outside the dugout like a pack of lunatics, and Ken, watching them, felt a great peace settle over him.

He was still a Terrier, and his hold upon that distinction was much more solid than it had been sixty seconds ago.

Fuzz Bankhead got a clean single over second, and Ken loafed across the plate, trying to keep his face blank as he reached the dugout. It was a hard job when confronted by the grinning welcome of the Terriers.

He took his seat and talked severely to himself. He had hit a triple, sure enough, but the game was young. All sorts of things could still happen, bad breaks, faulty judgment. "Take it easy, guy," he warned himself. "Don't let your head begin to swell. There are eight other guys in this."

Fuzz Bankhead stole second on the first pitch. Truck Hawley grounded out, and Bankhead went to third. Hal Mercer looped a long fly to center field. The center fielder nabbed it for the out, but Fuzz tagged up at third and came home after the catch. Bunker, maintaining the tradition of most pitchers, struck out to retire the side.

The Terrier fans made a hysterical fuss over their two-run lead, and the Terriers settled down grimly to protect it. They were successful for the next three innings, three innings packed with thrills and chills.

Both pitchers were standing the pace well, but the game was not a pitcher's battle. Both clubs were hitting, the Terriers trying to avenge themselves for yesterday's defeat, and the Rangers trying to prove the defeat was no accident. It was the sort of game that might go either way.

Ken weathered it to his own satisfaction. He did not get a hit his second time at bat, but he blasted a line drive that would have been a hit if the Ranger shortstop had been a couple of inches shorter.

Ken also made a couple of fancy catches in center field. It was significant that one of these catches, the one toward right field, brought on a brief attack of nerves. It was not because of the bright sun; his sunglasses took care of that. It was because of Cy Borg, whose bullheaded persistence in disliking Ken might lead to serious complications, particularly if a fly ball came to neutral territory where either man might easily catch it.

Proof of this was offered when a high fly headed for right center in the fourth inning. It was in Borg's territory, but Ken moved over just the same. That was routine, the accepted practice of backing up a neighboring fielder in case something went wrong.

Cy Borg was wearing the semi-automatic type of

sunglasses which fasten up beneath the visor of the cap when not in use, but which the player can drop promptly into position by a sharp tap on the visor. Borg tapped it, the glasses dropped into place, and he made the catch.

Then he turned on Ken and growled, "What're you doin' here? Did you think I'd miss that blooper? Stay out of my territory, busher. You're not welcome."

Ken turned and walked away without a word. But it worried him. He recognized this game as one of the high spots of his life. For the first time since he had played baseball he was enjoying a close intimacy with the other members of the team—with all but Borg. He forced himself to forget the incident and to keep his mind on the game.

That was not hard to do, because fireworks started in the top of the sixth inning. For the first time that afternoon the Rangers began to bunch their hits, with disastrous results.

They began with two singles, putting men on first and second. The third man laid down a sacrifice bunt in order to put both runners in scoring position. He did just that, and better. Mercer fielded the bunt along the third-base line, but the throw to first was wide. It pulled Flynn off the bag and all three men were safe—bases full, no outs.

Tobin walked in to talk to Bunker, but he did not take him out even though the warm-up signal had been sent to the bullpen pitchers. Bunker still seemed full of confidence, a matter that did not impress the next Ranger batter. The man singled to bring in a pair of runs and tie the score, 2–2. There were men on first and second with no one out.

That was all for Bunker. Tobin sent him to the showers, and Ken was pleased to see the long figure of Beezer Crane ambling from the bullpen. It was a tough spot for a rookie pitcher, but Beezer seemed quite unperturbed.

The first Ranger to face him laid down another bunt. Flynn, expecting it, was there to grab it. Fuzz Bankhead covered first, and the Ranger was retired.

Beezer bore down and scored a strike-out. If Beezer could retire the side without a further score, it would be his game to win or lose, and Ken believed he could win it.

Ken counted, though, without the breaks of baseball. The next Ranger, attempting a mighty wallop, dribbled the ball between the pitcher and the plate. Beezer and Truck Hawley rushed for it. Beezer, seeing Hawley had the better chance, threw himself aside upon the ground. Hawley made the play and got his man at first to retire the side.

But Beezer got up slowly, stood erect, and tested his left knee. He had bruised it in the fall, not badly but enough to put him temporarily out of service.

The Terriers tied to break the deadlock in their half of the sixth but the game entered the seventh inning, still 2–2.

Hank Schmidt, the big Terrier right-hander, took the mound. The first man singled. The next man, Sam Dillon, sacrificed him down to second, and the head of the Ranger batting list came up. A surprise bunt was successful, putting men on first and third. The man on first stole second, putting two Rangers now in scoring position. The next batter drew a deliberate walk to set things up for a possible double play. A pop-up to the infield accounted for the second out, but the situation was still packed with danger. The cleanup hitter, Harry Cord, was at the plate.

Cord was dangerous but Schmidt pitched to him. Cord swung with everything he had, but undercut the ball. It was a high, soaring fly to right field and Borg moved under it. A massive, relieved grunt came from the Terrier fans.

Ken, starting automatically to back up Cy Borg

on the play, almost checked his stride when he remembered Borg's frame of mind. Then he thought, "Nuts to Borg! Let him get sore if he wants to. My place is underneath that ball."

So he started for the spot, his long legs covering the ground with all their speed. He was still some twenty feet away when he saw disaster hit Cy Borg with stunning force.

Borg was slapping at the visor of his cap, buffeting the visor with savage helplessness. He was trying to dislodge his glasses, but they were stuck. They would not drop down so that he could look up into the white glare of the sun which hid the ball. The ball was coming at him but Borg couldn't see it. Ken heard a groan jerk from his throat.

Ken knew he had no chance to thrust Cy Borg aside and make the catch. But he watched the ball just the same, balancing his body as he ran, hoping for a miracle.

The ball crashed hard against the muscles of Borg's shoulder and bounced clear. It hung an instant in the air, then dove abruptly for the ground. But Ken Holt's dive was faster than the ball's. Ken whipped his body through the intervening space, his gloved hand stabbing for the ball. He reached it and hit the ground flat on his chest, but the ball stayed in his mitt. The first-base umpire was near enough to vouch for it.

He climbed to his feet, slightly winded. The fans were in hysterics. He lobbed the ball in toward the diamond, then turned to face Cy Borg.

Borg was staring at him with a dazed expression. He opened his mouth, then closed it. He turned abruptly and started for the dugout. He walked a half-dozen steps, then wheeled with slow deliberation and came back to Ken, his face a turmoil of emotions.

"I've got to thank you, Holt."

"Skip it."

"No," said Borg, shaking his head doggedly, "I can't skip it. You saved me from at least a two-run error. Why did you do it, Holt?"

"I didn't try to save *you* from anything," snapped Ken. "Just think it over."

He started for the bench. Cy Borg kept pace with him.

"Ken," Borg said, "I've been a pig-headed ape. I've had you wrong, and didn't have the brains to know it."

"Maybe you didn't have me so completely wrong," Ken answered.

"We'll skip that. Do we start from scratch?"

"From scratch," conceded Ken.

It seemed to be the missing segment of the jigsaw pattern. Fitted in, it transformed baseball into a perfect picture for Ken Holt.

He may have taken this belief with him when he went to bat that inning or perhaps he was just lucky. He hit a home run with a man on base. The inning ended with a score of 4–2.

The Rangers fought back viciously, still showing power. They pushed across another run in their half of the eighth. They were still in the ball game, still thoroughly dangerous.

The Terriers, knowing this, tried to increase their skimpy lead in their half of the eighth. They got a man as far as third, but he expired there when the next man grounded out to short.

The Rangers came in for their last desperate try. They were a fighting bunch, well disciplined and full of courage. The pitcher, scheduled to bat first, was replaced by a pinch hitter who came through with a single to short left.

The next man sacrificed him down to second. The Rangers intended to tie the score, if possible, and worry later about a win. The third man smashed a sizzling grounder deep behind first base. Flynn made a magnificent stop, but was too far off balance to make the out, even though the pitcher was covering the bag. Men were safe on first and third. One out.

The next pitch almost got away from Hawley. It was not quite a wild pitch, but it was in the dirt and required a body block. He held the man on third, but the man on first went down to second. A hit would probably score two men; a long fly would certainly score one.

The next Ranger relieved some of the Terrier tension by popping an easy foul to the first baseman. Things looked better now but were still too dangerous for comfort when the cleanup hitter, Harry Cord, came to the plate. He could hit to any field, so the fielders played him straightaway.

Schmidt worked on him hard but carefully and the count went again to three and two. Then he threw a fast curve. Cord had the break figured to a hair. He swung from his toes and connected. Ken saw the flash of the ball, heard the crack of the bat, and the next instant was sprinting wildly for the bleachers.

Fear rocketed through him as he ran, fear that he might never get his hands upon that ball. It was a mighty wallop. The briefest glance had told him that.

He was guided by instinct now. He had to trust

to his sixth sense that the ball would drop exactly where he believed it would. He dared not risk a backward glance. He couldn't spare the time.

The wall of the bleachers was upon him when he turned. He whirled and leaped at the same time. His eyes caught the briefest flash of white. He shot his glove toward it. He felt the impact of the ball in the pocket of his mitt. His fingers clamped down savagely. The next instant he crashed brutally against the wall. A wave of darkness swirled around him.

He fought his way out of a deep, black pit to find a group of anxious faces hovering over him. He raised his gloved hand with effort. The ball was gone. Black misery showed itself upon his face, but Cy Borg was there to put him straight.

"You *held* it, you fieldin' fool," he grinned. "We had to pry it from your mitt. How do ya feel, kid?"

Ken felt all right—after he had heard the welcome news. He was slightly shaken as he regained his feet, but otherwise no worse for wear.

He was surrounded by hilarious teammates as they all made their way toward the clubhouse through the crowd that had swarmed onto the field. But a small hurricane fought its way to the center of the group. It was Butch Browski, pop-eyed with excitement.

"Mr. Holt!" he yelled. "Hey, Mr. Holt! I just want to tell you the Busters could lick the *Terriers* now!"

"I'll say they could, kid," Ken grinned down at him. "Not only that, but maybe the Terriers would like to come and watch you lick the Bearcats."

The Terriers seemed to think it was a fine idea.